"I had hoped to help with Owen last night, but I never heard him cry."

Seth Bryant turned from the kitchen counter and caught his ex-wife's gaze. "I can't believe he slept through the night."

"He didn't." Lucy smiled at Seth as if she knew some great secret, which unfortunately triggered about eight powerful memories of when she'd given him that same smile—all of them sexual— and more than Seth's chest tightened this time.

The one thing his buddies hadn't factored into all of their instructions to prove to Lucy that he could be a good dad was that Seth had to be around Lucy. He hadn't *ever* been around this woman for a full twenty-four hours without making love to her....

Dear Reader,

To me, September is the cruelest month. One minute it feels like just another glorious summer day. And then almost overnight the days become shorter and life just hits. It's no different for this month's heroes and heroines. Because they all get their own very special "September moment" when they discover a secret that will change their lives forever!

Judy Christenberry once again heads up this month with *The Texan's Tiny Dilemma* (#1782)—the next installment in her LONE STAR BRIDES miniseries. A handsome accountant must suddenly figure out how to factor love into the equation when a one-night stand results in twins. Seth Bryant gets his wake-up call when a very pregnant princess shows up on his doorstep in *Prince Baby* (#1783), which continues Susan Meier's BRYANT BABY BONANZA. Jill Limber assures us that *The Sheriff Wins a Wife* (#1784) in the continuing BLOSSOM COUNTY FAIR continuity, *but* how will this lawman react to the news that he's still married to a woman who left town eight years ago! Holly Jacobs rounds out the month with her next PERRY SQUARE: THE ROYAL INVASION! title. In *Once Upon a King* (#1785), baby seems to come before love and marriage for a future king.

And be sure to watch for more great romances next month when bestselling author Myrna Mackenzie launches our new SHAKESPEARE IN LOVE miniseries.

Happy reading,

Ann Leslie Tuttle
Associate Senior Editor

Please address questions and book requests to:
Silhouette Reader Service
U.S.: 3010 Walden Ave., P.O. Box 1325, Buffalo, NY 14269
Canadian: P.O. Box 609, Fort Erie, Ont. L2A 5X3

Prince Baby

SUSAN MEIER

**Bryant Baby
Bonanza**

SILHOUETTE *Romance*®
Published by Silhouette Books
America's Publisher of Contemporary Romance

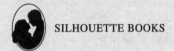 SILHOUETTE BOOKS

ISBN 0-373-19783-7

PRINCE BABY

Copyright © 2005 by Linda Susan Meier

This edition published by arrangement with Harlequin Books S.A.

® and TM are trademarks of Harlequin Books S.A., used under license.
Trademarks indicated with ® are registered in the United States Patent
and Trademark Office, the Canadian Trade Marks Office and in other
countries.

Visit Silhouette Books at www.eHarlequin.com

Printed in U.S.A.

Books by Susan Meier

SUSAN MEIER

is one of eleven children, and though she's yet to write a book about a big family, many of her books explore the dynamics of "unusual" family situations, such as large work "families," bosses who behave like overprotective fathers, or "sister" bonds created between friends. Because she has more than twenty nieces and nephews, children also are always popping up in her stories. Many of the funny scenes in her books are based on experiences raising her own children or interacting with her nieces and nephews.

She was born and raised in western Pennsylvania and continues to live in Pennsylvania.

Chapter One

Roaring thunder from a severe mid-September storm shook the windows of Seth Bryant's enormous two-story brown brick house in Porter, Arkansas, but that didn't prevent him from hearing the scream coming from his driveway. He bounced from his tall-back black leather chair and bounded out of his office, running up the slim corridor that led to the entryway.

When he reached the front window, he lifted the curtain, peering out into the darkness. In the muted glow of the lamp by his door, he saw Lucy Santos—*Princess* Lucy Santos—standing on his front stoop, and his look of concern shifted into a look of shock. He couldn't stop the painful thud that seized his heart. Even wet and windblown she was beautiful. Her dark hair had been tucked under a navy-blue rain hat that matched the huge navy-blue raincoat she wore, but he could see her long, shapely legs. That easily conjured a vivid picture of what the rest of her looked like. Naked. In his bed.

Cursing himself for being an idiot, he dropped the curtain and strode to the hall closet where he extracted his shotgun. Lucy might appear to be alone, but he knew better. Undoubtedly, two bodyguards lurked in the shadows, and even if she somehow had managed to escape them for the night, her chauffeur, Tony, a guy about half the size of a travel trailer, would be with her.

Seth cocked the gun. There was no way in hell she was getting into his house—his life. He didn't even want her on the same planet with him!

Aiming the shotgun with his left hand, he opened the door with his right. Shirtless and barefoot, dressed only in threadbare jeans, and pointing a weapon, he knew he probably looked like her royal bodyguards' worst nightmare. A crass commoner with a firearm. He smiled. It was too bad King Dad wasn't here to see this.

"What do you want?"

"Seth!" Lucy said his name like a gasp, then—as if she didn't see he had a loaded gun—she fell against him.

He caught her with his free arm but not before her cheek pressed into his bare chest. Shivers of joy ricocheted through him, but he gritted his teeth and squelched them. She'd brought him more pain than joy, and ultimately more anger than pain. He didn't want *anything* to do with this woman.

He nearly shoved her away from him. Then her weight and the shape of the body that collapsed against him caused him to realize that her raincoat was huge because *she was pregnant!*

"Oh, this is rich!" he said, just barely keeping his voice from becoming a shout, though he silently savored his anger. He had earned it. She had disposed of their marriage with a quick, easy annulment. Now it appeared she'd hidden her pregnancy from him. He had every reason in the world to be furious.

He didn't intend to let her see she still had the power to move him, not even to anger, so he softened his tone. "You're pregnant! You...*Princess!*" he said the title like a curse, because to him it now was.

Rain sparkled on her smooth, pale skin. Gazing up at him with dark eyes that glistened, she drew a quick, shallow breath and said only, "Help."

The distress in her voice caused Seth to forget their fight and to remember that a scream had brought him to his front door. *Her* scream.

He glanced outside to confirm that she was without her bodyguards and he saw that she'd driven the little red Chevy she sometimes used to sneak out when she wanted privacy.

He peered at her pain-filled face. "Lucy?"

"I think I'm in labor."

"Oh, my God." Before Seth could prevent it, a protective instinct rose up in him. As quickly as he could, he carefully leaned his shotgun against the wall, scooped Lucy into his arms and carried her across the pale tile floor of his entryway, through the dining room and into the living room where he deposited her on his white sofa.

"Not here!" Lucy groaned. "This is your living room!" Her eyes bore into his. "If I'm really in labor, we'll ruin your sofa!"

Seth scowled and he set her down anyway. Damned princess! "Even in pain, you're worried about possessions."

"I'm not worried about possessions! I'm being practical. You used to like that about me." She blew her breath out in three quick puffs, then ran her trembling fingers over her forehead. "The contraction is over."

Realizing her problem wasn't life-threatening, Seth tamped down his panic and allowed his anger to return. Still, he didn't let any emotion to filter into his tone when he said, "While I call an ambulance, maybe you would like to explain what you're doing here."

Lucy drew a quiet breath. "Okay." Her voice shook. Her eyes stayed downcast. "I left Xavier Island when I realized I was pregnant. I needed to finish the mansion in Miami, but I also wanted time alone to decide what to do. In the end I couldn't keep your baby from you."

Seth snorted in disbelief as he picked up the receiver of the portable phone on the end table by the sofa. Eight months ago, she'd let her father's representative end their marriage. Now she expected him to think she considered his feelings? His interests?

"Yeah. Sure. I believe that. I also have some swampland that would make a perfect retreat for your dad. Lots of alligators."

"Seth," she implored, grabbing his hand. "I know things ended badly between us." She caught his gaze. "You also have a right to be skeptical. I *wasn't* going to tell you about the baby because I thought it best that we never see each other again, but…"

She broke off with a gasp, then groaned loudly.

Seth's knees turned to rubber again. "Lucy! Do not have this baby on my sofa!"

She squeezed his hand. "Seth, something is wrong. Everything's happening too fast… I'm not even due for four weeks! Otherwise, I wouldn't have risked this long trip!"

"I think your doctor may have miscalculated your due date."

She closed her eyes and, between pants of air, she said,

"That would mean I got pregnant the first night we made love… *Aghghghgh!*"

Ignoring the vivid images that assailed him when he thought of the heart-stopping passion that had propelled him and Lucy to the bed of his Miami hotel room before they'd even had their first date, Seth punched 911 on the phone's keypad. When the dispatcher answered, he said, "I have a woman in my house who is in labor."

"How far apart are her contractions?" the dispatcher calmly asked.

Seth faced Lucy. "How far apart are your contractions?"

Lucy panted a few times before she said, "I had one pain when I got out of the car. One when you opened the door. And now the pain is back. It hasn't even been a minute. It's almost like the contractions don't stop!" She drew a quick breath then groaned again.

Seth said, "There doesn't seem to be any time in between the pains."

"Hold on, sir, while I fix your location…" Obviously tracing his address from his phone number, the cool, calm and collected dispatcher said, "I have you listed as Johnson Road. You're not very far…"

Seth glanced at Lucy. When he saw she was gasping for breath, he said, "Just get someone here!"

"Sir, an ambulance is on its way. Stay on the line and I'll guide you through…"

Lucy cried out in pain. Seth squeezed her hand. "Hold on, Lucy. An ambulance is on the way."

"I can't hold on." She moaned in agony. "Oh, God!"

Seth fell to his knees beside the sofa. "Operator, things are not going well here."

"Relax, sir, and tell me what's happening."

Before Seth could answer, Lucy said, "I'm going to have this baby right now!" She slid down on his sofa, with her feet flat on the cushion and her knees raised. Every inch of her shook, as if she'd been standing in the cold for hours. Her raincoat crackled and crunched from the nearly violent movement.

Seth said, "Operator, she just said she's going to have this baby right now, and I believe her. I have two neighbors who are volunteer firemen." He knew the volunteer firemen had paramedic training because he had considered joining the department himself. "So I think I'm going to hang up and see if I can get one of them to come over."

He disconnected the call, and, phone in hand, ran to his office to get the number of the two brothers who lived down the street. Once he found it, he dialed quickly, then began running to the living room again.

"Mark," he said when the older of the two brothers answered on the third ring. "This is Seth Bryant. I don't have time to explain, but my ex-wife is having a baby in my living room. I need you right now! And I do mean right now!"

Without giving Mark a chance to answer, Seth clicked off the call and raced to the sofa again. Lucy lay groaning and Seth dropped the phone and started undoing the closures of her coat. "Let's get this off."

She nodded and he nimbly pushed the raincoat from her shoulders. When he began to ease it from beneath her, she caught his hand. "Don't! Leave it for damage control."

Seth laughed, but the laughter was more from nerves than humor. "Okay. Good thought."

Lucy groaned again, digging her fingers into the edge of the sofa.

"Hang in there," he said, straightening her coat beneath

her. "Everything's going to be okay. I called my neighbors who are paramedics."

Lucy said, "Okay," then panted a few breaths. Seth noticed that she hadn't stopped squeezing the cushion and knew that what she had said was true. There was no time between the contractions.

"Mark and his brother live three houses down," he said soothingly. "Nine chances out of ten they only have to jump into their shoes before they can jog up here. Any second now my doorbell will ring…"

She groaned again. Her knuckles whitened as she squeezed the sofa cushion more tightly. "Seth, I can feel the baby coming out."

Not giving himself time to think, Seth reached under her skirt to remove her underpants. He heard the doorbell and prayed it was Mark. "In here," he called, knowing he couldn't leave Lucy to answer the door. But the wind howled, drowning out his voice.

He positioned himself between Lucy's knees. "In here!" he yelled. "Come in!"

When he didn't hear the sound of his front door opening he shouted, "In here!" as the child pushed free. Quickly, easily, the baby slid from Lucy and landed in Seth's hands.

He just barely caught it. "Oh, my God!"

Mark and Ray ran into the room. Ray laughed. "Looks like we're here just in time."

Seth glanced down at the baby. *His* baby. *His* son.

A prince.

"Oh, my God."

Seth watched the paramedics roll Lucy and the baby out of his house, down the sidewalk and to the driveway where the ambulance awaited. As they guided the gurney into the brightly lit vehicle, Seth closed his front door and started walking upstairs to get a shirt and shoes so he could join them at the hospital, but he had a quick second thought.

When he entered his bedroom, he grabbed the cell phone he had left on the cherrywood dresser with his wallet and change and dialed the home number for his personal attorney. As Pete Hauser's phone rang, Seth walked to the window and pulled back the sheer curtain and saw the ambulance speed away in the rainy night.

"Pete?" he said. "This is Seth Bryant."

"Seth? What are you doing calling at—" he paused and Seth assumed he'd glanced at a clock "—eleven-o'clock on a Friday night!"

Seth winced. "You were already in bed, weren't you?"

"Of course I was! Tomorrow might be Saturday, but I still have clients."

Seth winced again. "Sorry, but I have a big problem."

"What's up?" Pete asked, instantly alert at the mention of trouble.

"I have a son."

"What?"

Seth took a quick breath. "Let me start at the beginning. Remember that I told you I had been married, but you didn't need to worry because the marriage had been annulled and neither one of us wanted alimony or a settlement?"

"Yes."

"Well, I was wrong when I said we didn't need to worry. My ex-wife's dad is a king…"

"Seth, is this one of your jokes?"

"No joke. The bottom line is that our marriage was annulled because Lucy was promised to someone else in a trade agreement…"

"Seth!"

"I'm serious, Pete. Hear me out. She was betrothed to someone when she was a child, and that's a commitment as binding as a marriage in her country. So when her father found out about our marriage he told her our marriage wasn't valid. She went to Xavier Island to straighten things out, but she never came back. Her father's representative came to my door one day with the annulment papers I told you about that essentially said the marriage never happened. But tonight she showed up at my door and she was in labor. She actually had the baby on my sofa. But that's not the point. The point is she's an honest-to-God princess. Ty and I might have a bit of cash, but I'm guessing we can't compete with these people."

"You're afraid she's going to take the baby and you'll never see him again?"

"Exactly."

"Okay, here's what you do. Whatever it takes, you get her to stay in this country while I research the law and locate your best grounds for custody."

"While you're researching, Pete, keep in mind that my son is the first grandchild of the only child of a king."

Seth's lawyer gasped. "He's an heir to a throne?"

"I'm guessing. I don't know much about royalty and monarchies. I couldn't tell you who gets to rule and who just waves from the carriage in parades. But I do know that Lucy is an only child, and I suspect that a baby's being first-born—to an only child—means something."

"Okay. I'll hit the books. You keep your princess here. In Arkansas, if possible."

* * *

"It's called a spontaneous delivery," the emergency room doctor said, slapping Seth on the back. "Next baby, you'll be ready."

"There isn't going to be a next baby," Seth mumbled as the doctor pushed open the curtain, walked out of the cubicle and disappeared when the drape fell closed behind him.

Rubbing his hand across the back of his neck, Seth faced Lucy. "So, the doctor wants you to stay overnight."

Lucy nodded and Seth watched her, working to control the myriad of emotions tumbling through him. He understood what Pete was saying about keeping Lucy in Porter, but what Pete didn't realize was that Seth was irresistibly attracted to this woman. They hadn't even left his hotel room on their first date. Hell, they hadn't even said hello. The day they'd met on the construction site for her father's Miami mansion, they had fought the sexual connection that sizzled between them for eight long hours. So, when she'd arrived at his hotel room to meet him for their dinner date, she'd fallen into his arms and he'd carried her to bed.

With the exception of time at the construction site, they'd spent the first two weeks of their acquaintance in bed. But that was good because that was how he'd talked himself out of thinking he was in love with her. He simply convinced himself it had only been lust and the thrill of spontaneity that had propelled him and Lucy to Vegas where they were married after only knowing each other a few short weeks.

Blaming their marriage on uncontrollable sexual chemistry made everything easy to understand and justify, but now she'd had his child. And all kinds of crazy emotions bubbled through Seth. He might not love her, but he was absolutely, positively back to being solidly in lust with her. Except now lust was peppered with appreciation for the staggeringly beautiful woman who had given him a son.

He was in deep trouble.

He took a quick breath and reminded himself that Lucy had also married him when she had been betrothed to someone else. She had rushed home when her father discovered their hasty wedding and that had been the end of their relationship. She hadn't taken Seth's calls, wouldn't see him when he'd traveled to her father's island. Her father had sent the messenger who'd told him their marriage had been annulled. So, yes, looking at her beautiful dark eyes, perfect pink complexion and sinfully rich black hair, he couldn't deny that he was sexually attracted to her. What man wouldn't be? Having watched the birth of his son, he also couldn't deny a certain amount of respect and appreciation. But after the way she had treated him, he couldn't love her. He *wouldn't* love her. It would be emotional suicide.

"And they'll have a room for you in a few minutes."

She closed her eyes and murmured, "Thanks."

"You'll get the baby once you're settled."

"Good."

Seth ran his hand along the back of his neck again. *This* was the reason their marriage had been a mistake. Physically, they were a perfect ten. But he couldn't remember a time they'd ever really talked.

Still, able to communicate or not, they had a baby. And he refused to let the monarchy roll over his parental rights. Xavier Island might be a small country, only one island of several off the coast of Spain, but Lucy's dad was a savvy leader who knew exactly what to do to keep his country one of the richest in the region. If King Alfredo wanted to, he could find a way to take Seth's son away from him. So Seth had to be one step ahead of him. That was the important thing right now.

"So…what do we do now?"

"I'm going home."

He was afraid of that. "Where, exactly, is home?" Realizing how hostile that sounded, Seth quickly amended it. He couldn't afford to make her mad. Lord only knew what she would do, where she would go. She'd already proved that when she wanted to, she could disappear.

"When I met you, you lived in Miami, then when your dad summoned you, you left for Xavier Island. You said you've been in Miami for the past few months, but you were supposed to be marrying a prince. Did you marry him? Do you live in some other kingdom I've never heard of?"

"Though my betrothal nullified our marriage, the pregnancy broke the betrothal. The barristers called it an act of God."

Seth snorted a laugh. "I'll bet King Dad loved that."

"When he discovered there was no sanction to the trade agreement tied to the betrothal, he didn't care."

Seth shook his head, unable to believe things like this still happened in a modern world. "Well, there you go. Marriage, babies, none of it matters as long as the trade agreement stays intact."

"Seth, I know you're mad," Lucy softly said, "and I also don't expect you to understand this, but not every country is as progressive as the United States and not every people is as independent. Some of us…"

"Your room is ready!" Popping through the canvas curtain, the nurse interrupted Lucy. She picked up Lucy's chart and made a quick notation, then said, "The guy behind me is Tom. He'll be the one taking you up."

The tall orderly in the green scrubs offered a salute.

The female nurse turned to Seth. "You should go home. Not only is your wife going to need her sleep, but you've been through the wringer tonight, too."

Hearing Lucy referred to as his wife sent a flood of overpowering emotion through Seth. He fought it by reminding himself that he and Lucy were absolutely one-hundred-percent wrong for each other and they had made a huge mistake in getting married. But the feelings wouldn't go away. He wanted to take her hand and whisper his gratitude. He wanted to kiss her forehead. He wanted to jump with joy and he couldn't believe he had to control himself. He wasn't entirely sure he would be able to keep it all inside.

Still, he had to. Lucy was a princess and he might not be a pauper, but he was a commoner. They had to decide custody and visitation before she returned to Xavier. But Seth's lawyer needed to research the law. Seth had to buy him time.

He glanced at Lucy. "Do you want me to go home?" he asked politely.

"I am tired. But there are a few things we need to discuss."

"And you can't discuss them tomorrow?" the nurse demanded.

"No. Please give Seth my room number."

The royally-proper-yet-still-sweet way Lucy gave the command sent Seth's heart on a roller-coaster ride. That was what had first attracted him about her. She was the wicked combination of sexy and sweet. So sweet, she made him believe there really was goodness in the world. And so sexy he forgot his own name when he was with her.

The nurse sighed and faced Seth. "Her room is four-seventeen. But don't come up right away. We'll need about ten minutes to get her settled."

Seth nodded and left. He headed straight for the nursery, glad to have a few minutes to gather his wits. He stared through the glass wall as nurses fussed over the little boy he'd brought into the world. Having conceived a child seemed unreal. Being the owner of the first hands to touch him, seeing him take his first shaky breaths, those were miracles.

He also had an overwhelming sense of gratitude to Lucy for having given him a son. But that emotion was what bothered him. He wanted desperately to hug her, to thank her, to promise her the moon. And it was stupid. He didn't want her in his life anymore, and frankly, she didn't want him in her life, either.

Hell, he wasn't even sure she'd *ever* wanted him in her life. They'd known each other a little over a month. She had probably awakened one morning completely appalled by what she had done and had grabbed the opportunity to end their marriage when her father had summoned her. Actually, she could have been so appalled that she called her dad to get her out of her mistake. For all Seth knew, she could have been the brains behind the annulment.

Still, he understood what Pete was telling him. If he let Lucy go, especially if she took their child to another country where her father was king, Seth might never see his son again.

He waited ten minutes as the nurse had asked, then knocked before entering Lucy's room. He made the mistake of allowing his eyes to meet hers. He saw the warmth and softness in her pretty brown eyes and felt the attraction, the passion. All the wonderful things they'd once shared.

Damn!

He reminded himself to fight the feelings and reminded himself that even if he were fool enough to get involved with her, she didn't want to be involved with him. They were a bad combination. She had apparently seen that first. And when she'd run home to daddy, the king had disposed of Seth as if he were a scarred two-by-four.

That sobered him.

"I was hoping you would stay in Porter for a week or two so we could hammer out a visitation agreement."

Lucy played with the cover on her bed. "Seth, there are a few things I need to tell you…"

"I hope one of those things isn't that I don't have any rights."

She shook her head. "No. You are the baby's father. You have all the usual rights. In fact, I would like to name our son after your father. Owen."

The gesture surprised Seth so much he nearly had to sit. "Why?"

She smiled. "I think it's appropriate. One of the few things I remember you telling me in our short time together was how much you had loved your dad and how much you had missed him after he died. You told me your brother Ty had worked very hard to make up for the loss, but you always felt it."

Well, if that didn't shoot a bunch of holes into his theory that they hadn't really talked, Seth didn't know what did. Still, when push came to shove, she'd regretted their marriage and dumped him. Even if they had talked, they really didn't *know* each other. And even if they spent time getting to know each other that wouldn't change the fact that they weren't getting back together. He now thoroughly mistrusted monarchies and she would be an idiot to give up her throne for him.

Hell, who was he kidding? She just plain *wouldn't* give up her royal status for him.

Fortified by the truth of that, he caught her gaze again. She smiled slightly, honestly. And he felt the pull of attraction again.

Damn!

"I don't know what to say," he said, bringing his thoughts back to her kind gesture.

"Don't say anything. Owen is your son, too."

He took a breath, praying for strength in dealing with this woman who was drawing him under her spell again.

"Unfortunately, any visitation agreement that you and I create will have to be approved by my father's barrister," she said, sending him crashing back to reality.

"I don't see why," Seth said as anger spiked through him. He wasn't upset about the fact that Lucy wanted a lawyer to represent her; he simply didn't like the counsel she had chosen. Her father's barrister. The royal lawyer. The one who looked out for the rights of the monarchy first. Not even Lucy. *The monarchy.* "Why don't you just hire an attorney here?"

"Because that's not how it's done in Xavier."

"Well, honey, you're not in Xavier right now."

"I'm aware of that. However, you seem to be missing the big picture. Your son isn't just your son. He isn't even simply my son. He is Xavier's next king. And Xavier has a say in what goes on in his life."

Seth stared at her. "Are you kidding me? You're telling me that some guys in long black robes, probably wearing powdered wigs, are going to dictate how I raise my son?"

"Not dictate," Lucy insisted. "But they will participate in things like his baptism, where he will also be consecrated as Xavier's next sovereign."

"Is that anything like selling your soul to the devil?"

"Seth, please. It's a ceremony. There will be approximately ten or twelve ceremonies Owen will be required to attend. Until his coronation, when he will live in Xavier."

Seth combed his fingers through his hair, mad at himself for getting angry with her, but knowing he'd panicked because the last royal decree of her country's sovereign had destroyed their marriage and God only knew what the monarchy would do to an innocent little boy destined to be king.

Seth suddenly realized that controlling himself around Xavier's beautiful princess wasn't the only challenge he faced. He also had to fight for Owen's rights. If he didn't do something, there would be no Little League for his son, no mountain adventures, no cabins, cars, dates… Hell, his son might not even go to high school! Who knew what school a future king would have to attend.

Somehow or another, over the next few weeks Seth had to figure out a way to keep Owen in America.

Because if he didn't, Owen Bryant would end up like his princess mother, controlled by the wishes and whims of her country. And that was the real bottom line. That was what had hurt Seth the most. When Lucy was told she couldn't get married because she was already betrothed, she hadn't fought to get out of the betrothal. She'd simply left him.

That was why he could never lose an inch of his heart to this woman again.

Chapter Two

"I thought you were taking me to a hotel," Lucy Santos said quietly, as she glanced at Seth's brown brick house. Seated in the back of his SUV with her son who was sleeping soundly in his infant car seat, she caught Seth's gaze in the rearview mirror.

Seth tapped his fingers on the steering wheel. "I brought you here because I think it's smarter for you to stay with me than to get a hotel room."

Smarter? Lucy almost laughed as she considered the man she'd decided to marry in less time than she typically spent choosing a gown for one of her father's formal affairs. This morning Seth wore a pale green Polo shirt that brought out the green of his eyes, khaki trousers and brown loafers. But when she had arrived at his door the night before, he'd been wearing only jeans that hung low on his lean hips and she'd collapsed against his naked chest. At the time, she'd been in too much pain to register a reaction to his smooth, warm skin. But right now, she couldn't stop picturing the hard muscles of his torso, or remembering how nice it was to fall against the security of his strong body and realizing with sudden clarity why she'd married him after knowing him only two short weeks.

Tall and sexily slim, with sandy brown hair and unusual pale green eyes, Seth Bryant was gorgeous. But he was also a little rough around the edges. When she had met him and his older brother Ty at the site proposed for her father's Miami mansion, Seth hadn't known she was a princess, the daughter of the king building the magnificent home. Because she was an architect, he had assumed she was simply the project manager.

It was so nice to be treated normally that even though they'd fought over a few contract details, she hadn't told him she was a princess until after he'd invited her to dinner. Seth was bold, intelligent, and just rebellious enough to make her feel decadent. To a woman who had been sheltered most of her life, being with him was like living an adventure. They hadn't even known each other twelve hours before they had fallen into bed.

So, no. She didn't think it "smarter" for her to stay here rather than at a hotel, but their attraction to each other wasn't the most important thing to consider in this situation. Before Lucy took Owen home to Xavier Island, she also needed to know how to care for him without the help of a nanny. Her own mother, Queen Marianna, had died unexpectedly when Lucy was six. Lucy had felt more empty than sad, as if she hadn't really known her mother, and she refused to curse her son to that fate.

But if she didn't know how to care of Owen before she returned to Xavier Island, her father would insist on around the clock nannies. Lucy knew she'd never get to mother Owen unless she learned everything she needed to know before she went home, and to do that she needed a block of time with her son completely to herself. And in Porter, Arkansas, she was totally on her own.

As long as she called her dad and let him know Owen had been born and she was fine, her dad wouldn't panic and come looking for her. He might covertly station a bodyguard or two in Porter. But he wouldn't show up at Seth's door. He couldn't leave Xavier because on Monday Xavier's legislature went into session and there was no way he could cancel or postpone it without causing a stir.

They'd managed to keep Lucy's pregnancy a secret by saying she was in Miami working on the mansion. But if the king canceled the legislative session, the curious media would follow him to Arkansas. They would discover not only Lucy and her baby, but also Seth—a man unprepared for a deluge of reporters with questions about their marriage and the baby he didn't know he was having. Which meant a story her father's people could very easily control on Xavier Island would become a circus.

So, for the sake of making the facts surrounding the conception of Xavier's next king appear to be normal or even irrelevant, her father would attend the legislative session as if nothing were wrong. When the session was completed, he would travel to Arkansas and take Lucy and Owen back to Xavier Island with him, where his people would "spin" Owen's conception and birth to a situation befitting a king. But that would be okay. By then, Seth and Lucy would have decided visitation, and Lucy would know how to care for Owen.

The question was, was it better to be alone in a hotel or

in a house with someone who might be able to help her, but to whom she was also unreasonably attracted.

"How can you think my living with you is smarter than staying at a hotel?"

Seth turned on the front seat to face her. "You just had a baby. You shouldn't be alone. You need someone at least hanging out with you to make sure everything really is okay."

"Seth, the hotel staff would be a phone call away. Besides, I'm fine."

"Well, how about this, then? This period that we've agreed to spend deciding my place in Owen's life would be a good time for me to bond with him."

Lucy frowned. That was a much better argument than Seth knew. This wasn't merely a "good" opportunity to bond with his son. It might be the last such opportunity he would ever have. As the future sovereign of a small country, Owen would be living across an ocean. No matter how craftily Seth negotiated, Lucy couldn't promise him he would see his child any more than a few times a year, and those times would be at the palace, not at Seth's home. She had nearly told Seth that the night before at the hospital, but he looked so shell-shocked from the surprises he'd already experienced that she didn't have the heart.

She glanced at Seth's elegant house, beautifully detailed with black lanterns at the entryways and lining the stone walk to the front door. The two-story dwelling was big enough that she and Seth could probably live together for a few weeks without too many complications.

Particularly since Lucy wasn't worried that Seth was trying to wiggle his way into her life again. When she'd left him, he had been furious that she had dropped everything because her father had summoned her and livid that her royal responsibilities and duties took precedence over anything in her life—even him. When he didn't return her calls, it was only logical to assume he had regretted his decision to marry a royal. When he didn't protest their annulment, she considered it proof he had concluded marrying her had been a mistake. It had hurt at first. Actually, it had darned near killed her. But, in the end, she understood that Seth finally comprehended what she had been trying to explain to him from the first day she'd met him—it was not easy to be a member of a monarchy. And soon his son would be as involved as Lucy was.

It didn't seem fair to deprive Seth of this opportunity to get to know his son. Not when she could easily keep herself away from a man who had been glad to be rid of her, no matter how good-looking he was. "Okay."

"Okay," Seth said and pushed open his SUV door. "You get the baby. I'll grab his luggage."

Lucy carefully exited the SUV and reached in to unbuckle Owen and lift him from his protective infant seat. She nuzzled her nose against his velvet-soft face.

"Hello," she whispered. She was so full of awe and delight that this baby was hers that she almost lost her breath. After spending her entire life virtually alone, she had someone with whom she was irrevocably bound. Someone who would love her. Someone she could love without reservation, without fear of loss. Cuddling Owen closer, she squeezed her eyes shut and inhaled his sweet baby scent.

When Owen pressed his nose against her cheek, she knew he recognized her, and the power of instinctive love overwhelmed her again, nearly bringing her to tears and reminding her of how profound the loss of her own mother was.

"Ready?"

She faced Seth, wondering how long he had been standing there, but deciding not to make an issue of whether he'd seen her interaction with Owen. Even if he'd watched the entire time, she knew Seth wasn't looking at her as much as at the baby. Owen was his child and Seth was interested in him, not his baby's mother.

"Yes. We're ready."

She followed Seth up the long stone walk to the front door, but as he unlocked it, a black SUV roared into his driveway. The man Lucy recognized from working with him as Seth's brother Ty climbed out of the driver's side. A redhaired woman jumped out of the passenger's side. Clearly obsessed with getting to Seth, Ty didn't wait for his companion. His long footsteps had him rounding the SUV and striding toward the walk as Seth directed Lucy to the house.

In the foyer, she noticed the elaborate design of the pale orange tile floor and the elegance of the crystal chandelier that she had missed the night before. Seth hadn't had this house when they were married. But even if he had, they had decided to keep their wedding a secret until they figured out a way to explain it to her tyrannical dad. So Seth had never brought her to his hometown, let alone to his house.

"You have a lovely home."

Seth gave her a sheepish look. "I had to hire a decorator."

She laughed. "Really? A man who builds for a living had to hire a decorator?"

"I understand floor plans and designs and I can even approve or disapprove the details of an office building, mall or house, but I can't actually choose fussy things or match colors. God forbid I should have to pick all the frilly stuff for a bedroom."

Lucy stopped a smile. No, Seth wasn't much for frilly

things. When she thought of him in a bedroom, he wasn't mulling over the decor. He was naked, on the bed, in a tumble of sheets and bedspread.

The picture that formed in Lucy's head sent heat through her. She chastised herself for letting her thoughts go in that direction because she was absolutely, positively, through with this man. Nestling Owen closer, she glanced around, peering into the dining room, which was furnished with an oak table and hutch, and beyond that to the living room with hardwood floors and an elegant white sofa. "Your decorator did a beautiful job."

"Thanks. I took the liberty of having a crib and a few other essentials sent over. I set them up in the master bedroom."

An image of her and Seth on a bed with the baby between them appeared in her brain. Quick and perfect, the image filled her heart with the same kind of love she had just felt cuddling Owen. Her chest tightened and tingly warmth enveloped her. But on the heels of those feelings came pure panic. Not only did she not want to have these kinds of feelings for Seth again, but also his assumption that she would jump into bed with him was insulting!

Eyes wide, she spun to face him. "Seth! You don't think I'm sleeping with you! Because of my betrothal, we weren't ever really married. I can't… You shouldn't…"

"Don't worry, Princess. All that's behind us. I'm giving you the biggest room so you'll be more comfortable and so you'll have more privacy. I'll sleep in a guest room."

Relief poured through Lucy but before she could apologize for the assumption or thank Seth for the courtesy, Ty stepped into the open door of the foyer. Like Seth, he wore plain trousers and a short-sleeved Polo shirt, but the similarities stopped there. Seth had pale green eyes and sandy brown hair, while Ty had black hair and eyes so dark they could sometimes be described as black.

Ty said, "Hello, Lucy," then turned to Seth. "You're in trouble."

Seth said, "Hello, Ty."

"I didn't even know you and Lucy were dating! You can't imagine how shocked I was this morning when my future mother-in-law called me to tell me that her sources at the hospital noticed that my brother had a baby the night before!"

Lucy stifled a laugh at the exasperated expression on Ty's face, but Seth sighed. "Ty, Lucy is my ex-wife."

Lucy watched Ty's perfectly chiseled jaw fall. "*Ex-wife?* You *married* a princess!"

"Don't worry. There's no impact on Bryant Development…"

"No impact! If I remember correctly, we lost a ten-million-dollar contract."

"Yeah, well, that was all we lost. The marriage wasn't valid because Lucy was promised to someone else, so she wasn't free to make that commitment. It's as if it never happened."

Ty stared at Seth. "How can you say it's as if it never happened? *You had a baby!*"

"We did believe we were married for two weeks."

"You're in bigger trouble with Madelyn!"

Madelyn?

Lucy's chest tightened again, but this time it was from jealousy. Telling herself she wasn't jealous, only looking out for the interest of her baby by being *curious* about the people who would be around Owen for the next few weeks, Lucy eased the tightness with a soft, inconspicuous breath and glanced at her former husband. "Madelyn?"

"Ty's fiancée. The woman who's probably coming up the walk right now."

"And the head of public relations for Bryant Development," Ty reminded his brother. "How the hell is she going to spin this to make you look sane?"

"She's not. My private life is my private life. I don't see any reason this has to be 'spun' for anybody."

Ty sighed, then raked his fingers through his dark hair, as the red-haired woman entered the foyer. Lucy realized Madelyn had taken longer than Ty because she had retrieved a six- or seven-month-old baby. Wearing pink bib overalls and tiny tennis shoes, the little blond girl with the toothless grin was adorable.

"Madelyn Gentry," Seth said to Ty's fiancée as the baby she held merrily slapped her cheek, "this is my ex-wife, Lucy Santos."

Madelyn caught the little girl's hand, as if suddenly realizing she needed her full mental capacity. "Ex-*wife?*"

"Here we go again," Seth said, sighing.

But baby Owen made a mewling sound and he nestled more deeply against Lucy's breast. She glanced down to be sure everything was okay, and when she looked up, both Madelyn and Ty were staring indulgently at the tiny little boy.

Lucy smiled, proud of her gorgeous new son. "Would you like to hold Owen?"

Ty's eyes widened comically and he shrunk back. "I'm just getting accustomed to Sabrina."

"Your baby?" Lucy said, inclining her head in the direction of the little girl Madelyn held.

"Actually Ty got custody of Sabrina when his cousin and his wife were killed in a boating accident. So he's still learning the ropes," Madelyn explained, gently handing the little girl to Ty. "But I'm dying to hold Owen."

Lucy gave the baby to Madelyn as Seth said, "Let's go in the kitchen so I can make some coffee."

Ty and Madelyn followed Seth down the short hall by the hand-carved oak stairway, and Lucy followed them. She wasn't entirely sure she should be in on this discussion and as she reached the huge apple-green kitchen with the light wood cabinets, she decided she should take the baby from Madelyn and bow out.

Unfortunately, Ty was already talking. "And getting back to the gossip mill that squealed on you. You can expect Captain Bunny to be here any minute now."

Lucy glanced at Madelyn. "Captain Bunny?"

Madelyn clicked her tongue in disgust. "Ty calls my mother Captain Bunny because my dad is retired military, but my mother more or less runs the show in my house. So since my dad was a sergeant, Ty gave my mother a few ranks up and made her a captain. She seems to like that Ty recognizes she's in charge. The nickname is probably going to stick."

Lucy laughed. "Ty, I don't remember you being funny when I met you to discuss the terms of the mansion contract."

"I wasn't, but I'm changing."

He cast a loving glance at Madelyn and Lucy's heart squeezed with envy. She'd always known there was something missing from her relationship with Seth. *This* was it. She had loved that she and Seth were so physically attracted that they couldn't keep their hands off each other, but in the month they were together, there had been no private jokes. No intimate glances. No *closeness*.

She stopped her thoughts. The very fact that she and

Seth never got "close" was another proof that they were not meant to be together.

From the counter where he was pouring water into a coffeemaker, Seth said, "Ty, if you still have the list of prospective nannies you interviewed, I'd love to see it."

But Lucy shook her head. "I don't want my baby raised by nannies. I want to care for him. Besides, I thought the whole purpose of us being here was for you to have time with your son."

Busy adding the filter to his coffeemaker, Seth laughed. "Lucy, I might want to spend time with Owen, but I don't know how to care for a baby and I don't think it's something they taught in princess school."

She stiffened at the slight. She might be a princess, but she was a woman and she had all the normal motherly instincts.

"A woman who lived down the hall from me in Miami had a new baby," Lucy said, ignoring the insult to focus on the problem at hand. "When I realized I was pregnant, I asked if I could watch what she did and she let me. She taught me how to hold the baby, how to change a diaper, how to burp him. Then a nurse went over the basics again this morning at the hospital. Plus, I've read all the baby books. After a little practice, I'll be fine."

Ty shook his head. "Sorry, Lucy, but I'm afraid I have to side with my brother on this one. Your neighbor might have taught you lots of things, but you're going to discover there are hundreds of details she couldn't possibly have covered."

"Yeah, Lucy," Seth agreed. "Ty has had Sabrina since June. It's taken me three months just to get accustomed to holding her."

Lucy understood that she didn't know every little thing

about baby care. She also knew a nanny could certainly be very helpful. But a professional caregiver would also step in every time Owen cried and Lucy wouldn't have the opportunity she needed to learn to handle him by herself.

"I'm a quick study."

"So am I," Ty said. "Yet I had a hell of a time. Right, Madelyn?"

"Only because you didn't want to learn." Madelyn faced Lucy. "I think Owen needs a diaper change. You do have spare diapers, right?"

"We have the things we got from the hospital."

"Great. Let's go change his diaper," Madelyn said, nodding for Lucy to follow her out of the kitchen. "I'll take inventory of what you have, so I can shop for whatever is missing."

"That would be wonderful," Lucy said, as Madelyn guided her into the hall and then up the oak stairway. "Seth said he set up everything for Owen in the master bedroom."

"Good," Madelyn said, walking down the upstairs corridor. "You should have the best room in the house." She paused in front of the door and added, "I also knew we should get out of the kitchen before Ty bulldozed you into something you don't want."

Lucy laughed. "No one bulldozes me. Years of living with a king who is accustomed to everybody obeying him without question have taught me to handle just about anybody."

"I was hoping you would say that," Madelyn said. "But you're still going to have your hands full holding your ground with Seth." She glanced at Owen. "From the looks of things, you knew each other about nine months ago, and Seth has changed a lot since then. Don't expect to be able to sweet-talk him into anything. If he really wants a nanny, you're going to have a battle on your hands. And I haven't seen him lose as much as an argument in at least eight weeks. Not even to Ty."

Madelyn opened the door to the bedroom at the end of the hall. Stepping inside, Lucy gasped. Seth's decorator had to be the most talented person on the face of the earth. Not only was the cherrywood furniture exquisite, but also the airy green geometric print bedspread and drapes managed to be elegant and masculine at the same time. Lucy could imagine that with his green eyes, Seth looked delicious tangled in the sheets, and she found herself wondering if his decorator had chosen this particular fabric and color scheme for that reason. She wondered if he'd slept with the woman, and quickly realized that the creator of this room might even be why Seth never came after her.

She fought the molten jealousy that rose in her by reminding herself that she couldn't want a man who was totally wrong for her. Seth had deserted her. She'd actually had to debate whether he would even care to know she was pregnant! Worse, they disagreed about the nanny. Just like her father, Seth didn't want to be a hands-on dad. He would foist the raising of his child off to a stranger.

"I'm glad Seth isn't a pushover. Convincing Seth I don't need a nanny will be good practice for arguing with my dad."

Madelyn laughed. "All right. Just don't say I didn't warn you."

"I'm warned but I'm also very determined. My mother died when I was six, and because I was raised by nannies I never really knew her when she was alive. That will not happen with my son."

Eyes warmed with compassion, Madelyn nodded and said, "Good for you." Then she pulled off Owen's diaper, tossed it in the pail beside the changing table and reached for another.

Lucy studied every move Madelyn made. Though she had plenty of diaper experience from her neighbor's baby, and the nurse at the hospital had demonstrated even more basics, Lucy didn't think it would hurt to watch Madelyn to see if she did anything different, anything unusual, anything Lucy should know. In fact, now that she was alone with her son, she was beginning to feel a bit panicked. She could burp, change a diaper and rock him to sleep...but what if something else happened? What if he got sick? What if he choked! Dear God! She didn't know enough to be *alone* with this child!

Madelyn glanced over at her. "Are you okay?"

Lucy swallowed. "Sure."

Madelyn studied Lucy for a second, then said very carefully, "In spite of what you told Seth and Ty, you really don't know a whole heck of a lot about caring for a baby, do you?"

Fighting her panic because she didn't want Madelyn to see it, Lucy shrugged. "I lived next door to somebody with a baby..."

"I know and the nurse at the hospital also showed you a lot of the basics," Madelyn interrupted Lucy by finishing her sentence for her. "But, Lucy, Ty had a point. Things are going to come up that they didn't cover." She caught Lucy's gaze and very kindly said, "You need some help."

Lucy drew a breath. "Okay. You're right. But I don't want a nanny. I don't want somebody who is going to step in before I can when Owen cries." She drew another quick breath. "At the same time, I'm scared to death."

Finished with the diaper, Madelyn slid Owen's sleeper

into place and began snapping the closures. "How long are you planning to stay?"

"In the U.S. or here at Seth's house?"

"Here. With Seth."

"I don't know." Lucy hedged, not wanting to explain that how long she stayed depended on how quickly her dad could close the legislative session. "Seth and I weren't specific. We only agreed I would stay here while we talked about the visitation schedule. That would also assure that he has some time to get to know Owen."

Madelyn lifted Owen from the changing table and cuddled him against her. "So, technically you could stay in this house indefinitely as long as you never come to terms on visitation?"

Confused, Lucy said, "I guess, but my father's not going to let Owen live here forever and I don't want to give Seth the wrong idea."

"You won't stay long enough to give Seth the wrong idea. Only long enough for his neighbors to teach you how to care for Owen."

Lucy peered at Madelyn. "Seth's neighbors?"

"The way I see this, you can't let Seth know you can't care for this baby or he's going to get a nanny and then you probably won't get the experience you'll need to convince your dad you can care for Owen alone."

Lucy nodded.

"But I can't come here every day and help you. Seth would get suspicious."

Lucy nodded again.

"But, every day while Seth is at Bryant Development, one of my mother's friends could drop by under the guise of meeting the newest member of Seth's family. And while she was here, she could give you baby lessons."

Lucy pressed her hand to her chest. "It sounds perfect."

"It's *close* to perfect, but there is one potential glitch. To get the time you'll need, you can't have too much interaction with Seth or you'll come to terms on visitation too quickly and the next thing you know you'll be going home when you're not ready."

Lucy took a quick breath. "I can handle Seth."

She'd stayed away for eight long months and she could most certainly keep her distance for a few days.

The second the kitchen door swung closed behind Madelyn and Lucy, Seth faced his older brother. "We have got to get a nanny. I don't know a thing about caring for a baby."

Ty shrugged. "I'll send over my list."

Seth shook his head. "It is not going to be that easy. Did you see the look on Lucy's face when she said she didn't want someone helping her care for Owen? She'll fight tooth and nail before she'll let me get a nanny, but I need a nanny if I'm going to get custody."

"Custody? You're going to try to wrestle *custody* from a king?"

"Not from a king. From Lucy. When I called Pete last night before I went to the hospital, I only wanted visitation. But this morning I called him again and told him I want out-and-out custody and he told me that meant I had to change the way I was looking at this. We can't go at this from the perspective of Bryant Development against the monarchy. It's just me and Lucy deciding what's best for our son."

"I don't know, Seth..." Ty paused when there was a knock at Seth's back door. "That's probably Madelyn's parents," he said, grinning and shaking his head.

But when Seth pulled open the door, Pete Hauser stood on the threshold. Carrying about twenty extra pounds and going bald, Pete looked much older than his forty years.

"You have something already?" Seth asked, directing him into the kitchen.

"Not a precedent that gets you custody of your son," Pete said. "But I had two legal assistants from the firm's main office in Little Rock go online. They found virtually nothing on your princess or her country."

"It's a small island. I'm not surprised they found nothing—"

"I said *virtually* nothing." He handed Seth some papers. "This is a printout of the interview with Princess Lucy of Xavier Island from *Sophistication* magazine's Royal Issue. Did you know she didn't like growing up as a princess?"

"No," Seth said, slowly, embarrassed to admit in front of his older brother that he didn't know much about his ex-wife.

"Read the article. She talks about being raised by nannies and missing things like close girlfriends because she was educated at the palace. She laughs about never getting sent to the principal's office or having a chance to be a 'bad girl,' but if you read between the lines what she's saying is that her childhood was hard. Maybe too hard. She may not want her son to live that life, and while she's here you might be able to prove to her that with a 'commoner' for a father, Owen doesn't have to."

Seth glanced up sharply. "You think that if I play my cards right, she'll *give* me custody?"

"Not forever, but maybe until Owen is fourteen or so. Her childhood was what she missed. She didn't mind being royal once she got old enough to have a sense of responsibility."

Seth snorted. "Oh, she has a sense of responsibilities, all right. King Dad snapped his fingers and she went running home."

"That works in your favor, Seth," Pete insisted. "She knows how committed Owen will have to be when he gets old enough to assume his royal duties. So you need to show her that you could give Owen the normal life she didn't have in the only space of time in which he can have it. While he's a child."

Seth glanced over at Ty. "What do you think?"

"He may never join the family business, but at least we'll keep him out of purple tights and a fur-trimmed velvet robe until he's fourteen."

Seth laughed, but Pete said, "And when he's fourteen, we don't have to give him up easily. We can still file for custody. The trick will be getting the time right now to convince the princess that Porter, Arkansas, is the best place for Owen to have a real childhood. And that means you can't settle your visitation discussions until you've proved to Lucy that you will raise Owen in an absolutely normal environment."

Seth snickered. "Right. I wouldn't know a normal environment if it bit me in the butt. Once our parents died, Ty, Cooper and I lost our normal environment."

Ty shrugged. "Compared to Lucy's life, yours *is* normal."

Pete said, "Ty's right, Seth. Compared to her life, yours isn't that odd. You might have money, and your house might be big, but it's still in a quiet, safe small town where Princess Lucy's son probably wouldn't need a bodyguard."

"She hates her bodyguards."

"Exactly! So while she's living here, all you have to do is show her Owen would have a very normal life if he lived with you." He nodded toward the article in Seth's hands. "And whatever you do, don't even breathe the word *nanny*..."

"He already did," Ty said, "and she shot him down."

"Let the idea stay down, Seth. She talks in the article about not knowing her mother because she was raised by nannies, and I think that's your key. She does not want this kid raised by a nanny. So you have to learn how to change a diaper, take your turn getting up with Owen at night, feed him when he cries. And when you're not doing those things, make dinner, keep the house clean and do laundry."

Seth's eyes widened. "I have a maid..."

"Give her a paid leave." Pete turned to the kitchen door. "Your assignment for the next few weeks is to pretend you are just an average guy in an average town, who will raise his son in an average home so he can be an average boy."

"Great," Seth said sarcastically. "Should be a piece of cake."

Chapter Three

Five minutes after Madelyn and Lucy returned to the kitchen, Seth's house began to fill with people eager to see the new baby. Seth was glad when Ty suggested they leave the noise and confusion and hide in the garage, but he was surprised when his older brother took Sabrina from Madelyn's arms and also asked Madelyn's dad to join them. It wasn't until Ty returned from a side trip to his SUV with Sabrina's diaper bag and spread a clean blanket on an empty worktable that everything came into focus for Seth.

"Penney might be the Gentry family strategist," Ty explained, referring to his future mother-in-law. "But Ron was a sergeant and he knows all about boot camp and basic training. So he's going to teach you how to care for a baby."

Ron laughed. His once brown crew cut had grayed but he still had the muscular arms and chest of someone in the military. In under a half hour, using Sabrina as a model, he taught Seth enough baby-care basics that he could change a diaper, feed a bottle and burp with the best of them.

But Ron didn't stop there. "If your objective is to demonstrate to Lucy that you can give your son a normal life," Ron said, sounding as if he was briefing troops for a battle, not preparing a new dad for an encounter with the mother of his son, "then you have to prove that parenting is a natural fit for you. That means you've got to be involved with Owen's care right from the get-go. So I suggest you take the baby from Lucy as soon as your company leaves. That will give Lucy a break and also prove you can slide into the role of dad as if you were born to it."

Seth agreed, but even though Penney and Ron, and Ty and Madelyn and most of the morning guests left just after noon, a steady stream of visitors—women from one end of Porter to the other who came bearing gifts—never stopped. Seth didn't get two minutes alone with Lucy or his son. Forget about generously caring for Owen to give Lucy a break. There were so many women ogling Seth's baby that even Lucy didn't get to hold Owen. That evening, a small crowd actually gathered to get the baby ready for bed. Seth was lucky he got to kiss his son good-night before they hustled him out of the room.

But Seth didn't panic. If he wanted Owen to play in Little League, have friends, walk the streets of a town without fear or paparazzi, then he had to prove to Lucy that he could take very good, very normal care of their son. So he sneaked into the laundry room with his cell phone and called Ron.

"Here's what you do," Ron said after Seth explained why their original plan hadn't worked. "Owen's probably going to get up about ten times tonight. That doesn't sound like good news except by then, all the company will be long gone and Lucy will be alone. So you'll get your chance to prove yourself. You don't want to look obvious by running into Lucy's room the first time Owen cries, but I'll bet she'll be damn glad to see you at 2:00 a.m. Plus, taking your turn with the baby is a very gentlemanly thing to do. Not only will you give Lucy a break, but also you'll show her that you intend to teach Owen to be a gentleman."

Liking the two-birds-with-one-stone strategy, Seth stayed awake until Owen got up the first time, around midnight, to make sure he could hear the baby's cries so he could take his turn. Confident Owen was loud enough to awaken him, Seth went to sleep. But in what seemed like only a matter of minutes, he felt the warmth of the sunlight streaming in between the slats of the lemon-yellow horizontal blinds on the windows of the spare bedroom he was using and he bounced out of bed.

It was morning! He'd slept through the night! He hadn't heard Owen cry!

He scrubbed his hand down his face, then jumped into jeans and pulled on a T-shirt before he grabbed his cell phone to call Ron. He wasn't a complete idiot, but with the exception of Sabrina, he'd never held a baby in his life. He'd also never dealt with a new mother. He could "guess" what his next move should be but he didn't think he could afford the risk that he would say or do the wrong thing and alienate Lucy even before they'd spent twenty-four hours together. It was better to be safe than sorry.

When Ron answered, Seth simply said, "I never heard Owen cry."

"Easy, there, big guy," Ron said with a laugh. "Don't

panic. You still have plenty of opportunities to chip in and help out. Especially in the morning."

"Yeah, right. The baby's in Lucy's bedroom. It's one thing to go in in the middle of the night when the baby's screaming and she'll be glad to see me. It's another to barge in in broad daylight."

"That's true, but you can turn the whole situation around if you bring her a cup of coffee. She'll think you're being a good host, but she can't hold Owen *and* drink coffee, so you offer to take Owen and finish whatever she's been doing, like feeding him or burping him or changing his diaper. And, voilà, you look like a natural at being a dad."

Seth said, "Okay," then disconnected the phone and scrambled down the hall. Unfortunately, even before he reached the middle of the back stairway that led to the kitchen, the scent of fresh coffee greeted him. Confused, he rushed down the remaining steps and found Lucy sitting at the table, holding Owen, as she flipped through the Sunday paper.

Perfectly perky, she glanced up and smiled at him. "I made coffee."

"I see."

She wore a pretty pink flannel robe with lighter pink pajamas beneath it. The color brought out the rosy hue of her complexion and complemented her shiny black hair, which, this morning, was sexily tousled as if she'd just gotten out of bed.

Seth's mind jumped back to their time together and the thirty or so mornings he'd seen her hair just like that, and his blood began to percolate through his veins. His chest tightened. His breathing all but stopped. Though eight long months had passed since he had even seen Lucy, his body reacted as if it had missed the memo that their marriage was over and—more important—that Lucy didn't want him anymore.

He ignored the surge of his hormones and the crackling of his nerves, and walked to the counter where he retrieved a mug. Pouring himself a cup of coffee, he said, "I had hoped to help with Owen last night, but I never heard him cry." He turned from the counter and caught Lucy's gaze. "I can't believe he slept through the night."

"He didn't." She smiled at Seth as if she knew some great secret, which unfortunately triggered about eight powerful memories of when she'd given him that same smile—all of them sexual—and more than Seth's chest tightened this time.

Taking a sip of coffee, he tried to regroup, but he couldn't seem to focus on anything but how absolutely gorgeous she was. Ron had insisted that the trick to convincing Lucy he would be a good dad was projecting an air of casual confidence, especially around the baby. But the one thing Pete, Ty and Ron hadn't factored into all of their instructions was that in order to prove to Lucy that he could be a good dad, Seth had to be around Lucy. He hadn't *ever* been around this woman for a full twenty-four hours without making love to her. Hell, they'd slept together the day they'd met.

How was it that everybody forgot that?

He winced into his coffee cup. Probably because he hadn't actually admitted that to anyone.

Hoping to get his mind back to the project at hand, he glanced at Owen, but the sweet way Lucy held their son sent a god-awful tender feeling straight to Seth's heart. Needing every ounce of his discipline to keep his hormones in line, he didn't have any control left to manage his intense, almost incomprehensible gratitude to Lucy for bearing his son. The plan might be for him to show Lucy that he could provide a normal life for Owen, but with his body bubbling with need and his emotions zigzagging from appreciation to awe, it suddenly seemed wiser to leave the room. And maybe call Ron, or Ty, or Pete…or *anybody* who had a deep, masculine voice, who wasn't wearing silky-looking pink pajamas.

"So, you won't care if I go to the den and take a look at a proposal for a bridge?"

She dismissed him with a wave of her hand. "Of course not. We're fine." She peeked down at his son. "Right, Owen?"

The sleeping baby never moved a muscle, but even if Owen had begun spouting the Gettysburg Address, Seth couldn't hang around. "Okay, then, I'll be going."

He strode out of the room and Lucy breathed a sigh of relief. Not only did Seth look cuter than she'd ever seen him in his T-shirt and jeans, but also it was nine-forty-five. Penney had arrived at five o'clock that morning to give Lucy the opportunity to grab a nap, but since Penney had gone two hours ago, the only way Lucy could quiet Owen was to rock him. She adored this sweet child. She loved cuddling and nuzzling him. But reality wasn't merely creeping up on her; it had invited itself into her world and planned to stay. Her arm was asleep and she desperately needed a break.

Luckily, thanks to a schedule created by Penney Gentry, any minute now Mildred Jenkins would be arriving.

Right on time, a sixtysomething woman in capri jeans and a navy sweatshirt appeared at the back door.

"Hi, Mildred."

Mildred stretched forward and kissed Lucy's cheek. "How ya doing, sweetie?"

"I need a shower and my arm is numb."

Mildred laughed. "For the first week or so, you're more or less stuck holding the baby because he's too young to let him cry himself to sleep, so your arm's gonna be numb a lot." She glanced around. "Where's Seth?"

"In the den."

"Great," Mildred said as she took Owen from Lucy's arms, careful not to wake him. Then she sniffed the air. "Go shower."

Lucy laughed. "Okay, Mildred, I get the hint."

"Oh, sweetie, I'm not commenting on your smell. I'm trying to see if you have a certain cologne or something that you use consistently."

"I have shampoo especially made."

"That's right! I keep forgetting you're a *princess*."

"That doesn't win me any favors with Owen."

Mildred laughed throatily. "I hear ya. But I know a trick to give new moms a break. I got it from my mom. Tomorrow, when Seth's at work, we'll wash some of Owen's blankets with a drop of your shampoo. Just enough that he'll faintly smell you in his crib. That might solve some of this problem."

Lucy's lips lifted into a smile. "That'll work?"

Mildred laughed. "Sure. Nothing helped with my kids better than the remedies my grandma passed down to my mom. Now go. Owen and I will be fine while you're gone."

Lucy did as she was told. She showered, making sure she used enough of her shampoo that Owen would smell it on her, but she couldn't stop thinking about Seth. Something about him that morning gave her the oddest feeling. She tried to convince herself it had been nothing but attraction, lust, something easy to dismiss, but the response had been too intense and profound to be plain old passion. She had had four wonderful weeks of exposure to passion. That particular sensation had been burned into her brain and she knew that this whirlwind singing through her veins was different.

Still, when she tried to figure out what she was feeling, she drew a complete blank.

She emerged from the bathroom and rummaged through the clothes she'd packed for the few days she had expected to be a quick visit to tell Seth he was about to be a dad. She longed to wear something pretty, but she didn't have anything pretty. She only had maternity clothes. In a way, that was good. Her tummy was still swollen and she had to be realistic about the extra few pounds she had put on while pregnant. And, after seeing Seth that morning, looking so unbelievably perfect in his jeans and T-shirt, Lucy was glad she wasn't up to par physically. With her attraction to Seth constantly surging to life, and the new unnamed sensation that had overwhelmed her that morning, it was a good thing to feel completely unattractive. This way, there was absolutely no possibility that she would forget herself and give in to the urge to flirt with him.

When she returned to the kitchen dressed in a pair of maternity jeans and a big T-shirt, Mildred was reading the paper, Owen on her arm. Seth was nowhere in sight.

"Did he come in?"

"Nope. And I made some sandwiches for lunch. Nothing fancy. Just tuna salad."

"Tuna salad sounds wonderful right now. But I thought you guys were only going to help with Owen."

"Mothering's more than caring for the baby." Mildred

rose from her chair. "If you really want to make sure Seth doesn't lose patience and hire a nanny before you've had enough time to learn how to care for your son, you have to make him see you can handle *everything* that pertains to this house on your own. Including cooking and cleaning. Since you've never really done anything like this, we're here to fill the gap."

Lucy relaxed. "Thanks. I'm glad Penney realized I would need help."

Mildred laughed. "Lucy, sweetie. You couldn't be in better hands. When Penney Gentry plans something, it works." She walked to the door, but before she opened it, she turned and smiled. "Audrey Olsen is scheduled for noon."

Lucy smiled appreciatively. "Thanks."

Audrey Olsen was a thirty-year-old woman who had recently retired from Bryant Development's accounting department to have her own children.

"It's been three months since I quit and I'm not pregnant yet," she told Lucy as she prepared a supper casserole at the counter by the stove. She hopped from cupboard to cupboard, choosing ingredients and her blond ponytail bounced perkily. "But three months is a drop in the bucket. I've got years." She paused, and her head tilted in question as she looked at the well-stocked cupboard. "I've never seen a man who had so many spices."

Watching Audrey bob from cupboard to cupboard, Lucy had seen all those spices, too; when she had, it had taken her at least twenty seconds to be able to breathe. After having had the unnamed feeling about Seth that morning, it was a slap of reality to realize her former husband didn't merely have spices he also had four different pastas and ingredients for sauces. Preparing Owen's bottles that morning, she had also noticed that Seth's fridge held fresh vegetables. She knew a well-stocked kitchen was a big deal, and that any spice beyond salt, pepper and garlic powder meant there was probably a woman in Seth's life.

Audrey chatted happily as she finished the casserole and slid it into the oven. Then she poured herself a cup of coffee and set it on the table, preparing for her time alone with Owen. "Okay. You go freshen up before we call Seth in for the sandwiches Mildred made," she said, rubbing her hands together excitedly as if she couldn't wait to hold the baby.

Lucy nodded. She refused to dwell on Seth with another woman. It would be foolish to think he *hadn't* found someone else in all the time they had been apart. Besides, she certainly didn't want to get involved with him again. He had committed to her, but the minute she was out of sight, he apparently had forgotten she existed. He had never so much as taken one of her phone calls, let alone thought of placing one himself.

No. She didn't want him. She and Owen would be perfectly happy without him.

But given that he was Owen's dad, Lucy also knew she had to adjust to seeing him—albeit only once or twice a year—for the rest of her life. When Seth arrived on Xavier Island to visit his son, it was also possible he could bring the spice girl who stocked his cupboards. Lucy might as well accustom herself now to the idea of Seth with another woman.

She rose from her seat to hand the baby to Audrey, but as she did, Seth pushed through the swinging door. Because he had showered and changed, he no longer wore the jeans and T-shirt she had seen him in that morning. Instead, he had on the same khaki trousers and dress shirt he had worn one of the days they'd spent at the site of her father's Miami mansion.

Lucy froze as disjointed details of that day rolled through her brain. The sun had been hot. Ocean waves had lapped behind them. She and Seth had been married. They were two people passionately in love.

The reality of it poured through her. They had really thought they were in love, but she had reduced the intensity of their feelings to "lust" because that made everything easier to deal with. Seeing him in those clothes resurrected memories and feelings that she couldn't deny or explain away. Feelings that made everything that had happened between them real again.

"Hey, Audrey," Seth said, easily accepting the presence of another "visitor" here to see the baby and bringing Lucy out of her reverie and back to the present. "What's up?"

"Not much," Audrey said, taking the baby from Lucy's hands.

"Are you staying for lunch?" he asked.

Seth turned to open the refrigerator and Lucy caught Audrey's gaze. Audrey nodded that it was okay, and cautiously said, "Yeah. That would be great."

"Good. While Lucy was busy with her company yesterday, I bought some deli meat and rolls. There should be pickles in the fridge. Want to get those out, Lucy?"

Lucy's breath froze, but she managed to bring herself around quickly. "Seth, I…" she couldn't quite lie and say she'd made the tuna sandwiches Mildred had prepared. So she amended her statement to, "There are already sandwiches made in the refrigerator. Tuna."

Mustard in hand, he stepped away from the counter. "Oh."

"Yeah, I didn't want to go overboard." She caught his

gaze. A symphony of butterflies fluttered in her tummy. Not because she hated lying, but from trepidation. When she looked into Seth's gorgeous green eyes, she always saw more than his words could ever convey. And right now, she could swear she was disappointing him. "You like tuna, right?"

"Yeah. Tuna's fine," he said quietly, his displeasure evident in his tone.

Lucy's chest tightened. She'd *never* disappointed him. She'd angered him. Confused him. Made him laugh. Aroused him. But *never* disappointed him.

Still holding her gaze, he said, "I just thought you might want some help…"

"Some help?" Audrey interrupted with a laugh. "Our girl Lucy is a natural! She doesn't need any help." Audrey waved her hand as if pushing his concern away. "Seth, grab a sandwich and get back to whatever it is you need to do. Lucy is fine."

He caught Lucy's gaze again. "Is that true? Are you fine?"

She really hated lying so she only smiled, hoping that would pass for an affirmative response.

Seth drew a quiet breath. "Okay, then."

When he was gone, Audrey sighed noisily. "That was a close one."

Lucy said, "Yeah." But the weight of Seth's disappointment nearly suffocated her. Now that the memory of their visit to the site of her father's Miami mansion had sneaked through her fortress of resolve to forget him, lots of other memories were sliding through, too. The most significant of them were recollections of Seth's interactions with his employees. The very day Lucy met him, she had easily deduced from the way he treated his employees that he was a good person. Honest. Sincere. Hard-working. Yet here she was, deliberately deceiving him.

But she was doing it for good reason. And most of that reason didn't pertain to him, but to her father. She needed to know how to care for Owen when she returned to Xavier. She wanted her son to know his mother. If she was deceiving Seth, it was for Owen. And she wasn't really lying, or even cheating. She was simply hiding information from Seth and that wasn't really wrong. It was more like self-preservation.

That evening Lucy was exhausted from keeping up the pretense with Seth. Caring for Owen wasn't nearly as tiring as thinking up good reasons for so many visitors—especially visitors who were helping make formula, tending to Owen's bath and keeping Seth away from his own son.

Still, all night she bounced out of bed every time Owen as much as whimpered. She didn't want Seth getting the impression she couldn't handle their baby. She needed this time to become competent at caring for Owen alone.

Monday morning when Penney arrived, Lucy was sorely in need of sleep again. But this time she and Penney didn't have to fear Seth awakening and discovering their plan because he was leaving for work soon. Lucy stayed awake while he got dressed, chatting with Penney, who came over in the guise of dropping off some baby clothes. But after he left, she went right back to bed and slept away the morning. When Audrey arrived at two, she felt much better. Far less in need of a rest and more in need of a lesson or two about caring for Owen.

"That's great," Audrey said, "but I'm the one without a baby, remember? I can keep a kid happy for a few hours while you nap, but I can't tell you all the great stuff Penney and Mildred know because of raising kids themselves. So, I guess what we need to do is shift me to mornings and have one of them come in the afternoon when you've got the time and energy to learn."

Seth picked that precise second to walk into the kitchen. "Learn what?"

Caught, both Lucy and Audrey looked over at him as he walked to Lucy to take a peek at Owen before going to the counter that held the coffeemaker. Because it wasn't any later than two-fifteen, neither one of them had expected Seth to return from work. Worse, he was dressed in a sweatshirt and jeans, as if he had been home for some time.

Audrey said, "Lucy was just going to run upstairs for a few seconds and I was assuring her that though I have no children of my own, I am perfectly capable of caring for yours for the ten or twenty minutes she'll need to shower or whatever."

But while Audrey spoke, Lucy sat transfixed. She understood why the familiar dress shirt and trousers from the day before had knocked her for a loop, but had absolutely no explanation for why the way he looked today was just as appealing. She supposed it was because in all their days in Miami, she had never really seen him look so casual or comfortable. She knew what he looked like naked. She knew what he looked like in a suit or even a dress shirt and jeans, directing a construction project when they had visited the site. But she'd never really seen him in casual clothes and it was beginning to overwhelm her. Not because he looked so male, but because he looked so normal.

That was it! That was the odd feeling she had had on Sunday morning! Seth didn't merely look normal; he also made her feel normal! Blissfully, wonderfully normal! Not like a princess, just a woman. She had somehow forgotten that the biggest part of her attraction to Seth was that around him she wasn't a royal. She was a woman. A woman he desperately wanted. Right from the beginning, she'd seen the spark of sexual attraction glowing in his green eyes and felt the answering attraction spiraling through her. It was pure. It was simple. And it had nothing to do with her as a royal and everything to do with her as a woman.

"Right, Lucy?" Audrey said, poking Lucy's elbow. "I'm going to hold Owen while you take a few minutes to freshen up."

Lucy drew in a quiet breath, wondering how long she'd been staring at her former husband and if any of the emotion she'd been feeling had shown on her face.

Audrey reached for Owen. "So, I'll take the baby."

"No," Seth said, walking to the table where Lucy sat. "Let me. Between the company we had on Saturday and the visitors yesterday, I haven't had a chance to hold my own son. I've lived here five months and never had a neighbor do more than say hello. But just put a baby in a man's house and suddenly every woman in town pops in for a look."

Lucy peered at Audrey and she shook her head slightly, as if saying Lucy shouldn't make too much of Seth's observation. Lucy nodded imperceptibly to show she understood, then loosened her hold on Owen as Seth took him from the crook of her arm.

Unfortunately, as he wrapped his big hands around Owen's tiny body, his eyes met Lucy's. What passed between them was stronger and more intense than the sexual tension they had always effortlessly generated. With their gazes locked and forearms brushing, Lucy recognized he was completely real to her again. He wasn't a memory of four weeks of reckless passion. He wasn't a guy she had worked with. He was the guy she had loved. Really loved. Loved with such passion and desperation she'd literally forgotten she had responsibilities to her country.

And if she didn't believe it to be completely improbable, impractical and in some ways just plain stupid, she would wonder if she didn't love him still.

But even if she did, it didn't matter. He had been furious when she'd returned to Xavier at her father's summons. When he hadn't protested their annulment, it was clear he regretted having married a royal. Not only that, but he'd already replaced her with the spice girl.

As if to confirm that he didn't want her anymore, Seth lifted Owen and quickly pulled away. "Audrey's right, Lucy. You do need a break. I'm sure she wouldn't mind cutting her visit short and I'm fine with Owen. Why don't you take a nap?"

Audrey nodded and said her goodbyes.

Lucy rose slowly. Reminded of her royal responsibilities, which had increased since she had become the mother of Xavier's future king, she knew she couldn't give Seth an opening to prove she couldn't care for their child.

Reaching for the baby again, Lucy said, "I'm fine."

"Okay, then, how about this?" Seth said, losing patience with her. "I'd like some time with the baby and I'm taking it. You do whatever you wish."

With that he turned and walked toward the kitchen door, but he stopped abruptly and faced her again. "Oh, and I'm making dinner."

"That's okay, Seth," Lucy began to protest, but Seth stopped her.

"You're a guest in my house."

"But I'm perfectly capable of making dinner."

Seth held his ground. "So am I. A person doesn't grow up without parents without learning to cook."

Though Lucy knew there was no future for them, understanding rippled through her. His parents had died when he was fifteen and he'd been forced to learn to cook or starve. That was why his cupboards were stocked.

There wasn't any spice girl.

"I forgot you'd lived on your own since you were a child," she said.

"With my two older brothers," Seth corrected casually. "But it still made me a hell of a cook. I can also clean and iron, but my specialty is cooking. No one would starve in my house."

Lucy couldn't help it. She laughed at the seriousness of Seth's tone. He was fighting her for the chance to make dinner. "All right, you can cook tonight, but just for the record, no one would starve at my house, either."

"Not when you have maids," Seth said with a chuckle.

She shook her head. "I don't have maids. In fact, I no longer have staff." She'd gotten rid of them to prepare everyone for seeing her caring for Owen on her own. "I had to keep my bodyguards, but otherwise I take care of myself."

Paused by the kitchen door, Seth held her gaze. "You take care of yourself?"

"We seemed to do pretty well without a staff the weeks we lived together."

The pained expression that came to his face confused Lucy. If it was so difficult for him to think of their marriage ending, why hadn't he tried to save it? "Seth, why didn't you answer any of my messages?"

He shook his head. "I didn't get any."

"Oh, come on. I couldn't get out of bed when the morning sickness and tiredness first hit me, but I sent you several e-mails through my personal assistant." In the last she had asked him—almost begged him—to meet her, but he had never answered, and that was why she stopped trying to reach him. In fact, that was why she had wondered if he even wanted to know about their baby. Getting involved with a princess clearly had been more than he'd imagined, and she was willing to let him off the hook since it appeared he wanted nothing to do with her.

"Never got them."

Which meant he never knew how desperate she had been to see him. A horrible possibility crept into Lucy's thoughts. There was only one person who could order her assistant not to send an e-mail. "Let me get this straight. You didn't get *any* of the e-mails I sent after I left?"

Seth shook his head again. The expression on his face changed from pained to aware, and Lucy knew he'd figured out the same thing she had.

"Just like you didn't get any of my messages, did you?"

She took a quick breath. *He'd tried to contact her, too.* "No. And don't even bother accusing my father. Before you say the words, I'll apologize for him. We both know he's the only one with enough power to order the staff not to send an e-mail or to have an e-mail deleted before I saw it."

Seth raked his fingers through his hair. "So you didn't just leave me high and dry?"

"I would have never done that. I wanted to see you." She had been aching to see him. Brokenhearted. Desperate. Hungry simply for the sight of him. And he might have been desperate to see her, too. "And you didn't dump me for your decorator."

Seth said, "What?"

"It's nothing," she replied, but she knew that wasn't true. Without the anger that had separated them, they were the same two people who had made love two hours before her plane left for Xavier Island that fateful January afternoon.

"This is why you kept the baby from me until the last minute, isn't it?"

She nodded. "When you didn't meet me as I asked in my last message, I assumed you had gotten back to your normal life. And I knew your normal life didn't include being the father of a future king. It was hard enough for me to accept that you didn't want me anymore. I couldn't handle having you tell me you wanted nothing to do with our child."

"I would have never told you that."

They gazed into each other's eyes and realization crackled between them in the silence that descended. A myriad of facts reordered themselves in Lucy's mind and took new meaning. Seth hadn't deserted her. He had tried to contact her. Their marriage hadn't ended because their feelings had died. Their marriage had ended because of her royal betrothal. And then, when the pregnancy nullified her betrothal, her father kept them apart to make sure they never remarried.

They now knew neither had wanted their marriage to be over. Remarrying wasn't out of the question.

The thought hadn't even completely gelled before Lucy knew that wasn't true. Seth absolutely hated the fact that she was royalty. Even if he still loved her, he wouldn't want anything to do with her. She was a princess and though at first Seth might have thought being married to a princess would be interesting, or fun, he now understood that she had duties and responsibilities. He bitterly resented that being married to him hadn't kept her from running home at her father's summons.

And even if he asked her to abdicate her throne, she couldn't do it. She was now the mother of a future king and bound by law and love to either train Owen to be Xavier's king or give him up to the monarchy.

So even if they loved each other as passionately as they had that January, marrying again was out of the question.

Her father had won after all.

"You know what, Seth, it doesn't matter how the marriage ended. The truth is, it's ended. And in a way that's best for both of us."

Chapter Four

The next morning, after Lucy had bathed Owen and was dressing him for the day, the phone rang. Realizing it was probably Audrey, who had forgotten she'd switched with Mildred from afternoon duty to morning duty and who was currently late, she answered the phone with a cheerful hello.

"I don't know what is wrong with me this morning," Audrey said, then paused and gulped in some air. "But I feel awful!" She paused again and took another deep breath. "Actually, what I feel is that I'm going to puke."

"Oh, Audrey! This is great!"

Audrey groaned. "Are you insane?"

"No! I think you're pregnant!"

"Pregnant?"

"You're feeling exactly how I felt the weeks before I took the pregnancy test," Lucy said, juggling Owen to her shoulder.

Audrey was quiet for a second before she said, "Oh, my God. I could be pregnant?"

"Yes!" Lucy said with a laugh. "And right now, I think you should go back to bed."

Audrey took a quick breath. "First, let me call somebody else to fill in for me this morning."

"No," Lucy said, glancing down at Owen. She knew how to handle all the routine baby chores. She'd also slept a fairly decent amount the night before. The lessons she now needed pertained more to "problem" areas and future events than basic baby care. But that could all be done in the afternoon. Lucy was positive she and Owen would be fine on their own this morning. In fact, if Audrey was pregnant, Lucy decided she could care for Owen by herself every morning. It would be good practice for being totally alone with Owen on Xavier Island.

"You just go back to bed. And don't worry about me. Owen and I are fine."

Audrey protested a bit, but Lucy held her ground and Audrey finally said, "Okay."

Lucy disconnected the call. She'd already made a pot of coffee but hadn't yet fed Owen. Walking down the back stairway, she heard Seth puttering around, getting a mug from a cupboard and cream from the refrigerator. She simply turned around and returned to her room rather than be alone with him.

Realizing the day before that her father had separated them had opened a whole new can of worms. Now that they both knew that they hadn't fallen out of love, their attraction hadn't diminished and neither one of them had dumped the other, they would face each other with an entirely different set of understandings than they'd had when they'd arranged for Lucy to live here. One or the other might even be tempted to test their attraction. And that would be wrong. If only because Lucy didn't even have to ask Seth to know he didn't want to be married to a royal. There was no possibility of reconciliation for them.

So she waited until Seth left to get Owen's bottle, and after that she easily fell into the morning routine of feeding Owen and rocking him back to sleep. Things went so smoothly she was tempted to leave Seth's home and get them both out of harm's way.

But Owen was only four days old and Lucy wasn't sure it was wise to travel. Plus, both Penney and Mildred had told her that there were hundreds of little things they needed to teach her about caring for Owen. So she couldn't leave. Instead, she would have to continue to find ways to keep her distance from Seth. At least until they both adjusted to the fact that neither of them was to blame for the demise of their marriage. And until they both realized that getting married again was not an option. And until they both realized that testing their attraction wasn't a good idea, either.

"Are you going to dress like this forever?" Ty asked, parking himself on the seat across from Seth's desk.

Seth glanced down at his sweatshirt and jeans, then leaned back in his soft brown leather office chair and propped his tennis shoes on the corner of his heavy mahogany desk.

"I thought I was supposed to show the princess I was a normal guy."

"You are, but this is your job, not a football game. Madelyn may have convinced me to relax the dress code, but I still don't allow jeans and sweatshirts in the office during regular business hours."

Seth said, "Fine." But only because he knew he could change into jeans and a sweatshirt the minute he got home. In fact, he intended to wear nothing but jeans and sweatshirts around Lucy for the rest of her stay because yesterday, when he had been dressed almost exactly as he was right now, she couldn't hide the fact that she was attracted to him.

Twice he had caught her staring at him. Once, she had even appeared to be speechless. Her eyes had become glazed. Her breathing had shifted. For the first time since she'd reentered his life the Friday before, it was patently clear that she was as attracted to him as he was to her. When he'd scooped Owen from her arms, he'd held her gaze and let his arm brush against hers, and sparks virtually had flown from her to him.

Plus, now that he knew she hadn't deserted him to be a princess and she knew he hadn't abandoned her, everything between them had changed. Not that he thought they would marry again; that wasn't in the cards. However, Seth wasn't averse to using any way or means to remind her he was one of the good guys. For four wonderful weeks, she'd thought the sun rose and set on him and he was sure he could make her feel that way again. If it took sweatshirts and jeans to get her to loosen up and to look at him the way she had in Miami, then so be it.

Reminding her of their attraction was the first step to reminding her that she had liked and trusted him. And that was the first step to getting her to see he was the best person to raise Owen.

Ty shook his head. "Why the hell are you wearing jeans and a sweatshirt anyway?"

Seth appreciated Ty's help with figuring strategy to get custody of Owen. He intended to keep his brother apprised of what was going on with Lucy, but he would only tell Ty the parts of the situation he needed to know. "I left work early yesterday, walked into the kitchen in these," he said, pointing at his sweatshirt and jeans, "and Lucy all but handed Owen to me."

"And that's relevant because…"

"Because I'm having trouble getting the baby from her. It's nearly impossible for me to even hold Owen—let alone prove I can care for him. I've been lucky to get to kiss him good-night with the nanny brigade that's been through my kitchen in the past four days."

"Nanny brigade?"

"There's a bunch of women who visit nonstop. Every time I turn around, one of them's hovering. Cooing at Owen, giving Lucy baby tips. I listened at the door once and overheard your future mother-in-law showing Lucy how to move Owen's legs as if he's riding a bicycle as a way to get rid of gas so he doesn't become colicky. If I didn't know better, I'd think Penney was actually holding classes for Lucy."

Ty scowled. "She most likely is."

Seth frowned. "You think Penney is teaching Lucy how to care for Owen?"

Ty shook his head. "If my guess is correct, this is much bigger than that."

Seth stared at his older brother. "What are you talking about?"

"On Saturday morning when you brought the baby home, Madelyn lured Lucy out the kitchen right after you mentioned you wanted a nanny and Lucy said she didn't.

At the time, I thought Madelyn had spirited her away to avoid an argument, and she may have. But in the process of spending time alone with Lucy, I'll bet Madelyn also got Lucy's side of the story."

"About why she doesn't want a nanny?" Seth asked, confused.

"Yes, and even though that's not a terrible thing in and of itself, Madelyn wasn't in the kitchen when Pete showed up, so when she was talking with Lucy she didn't hear *your* end of the story. Lucy might have even told Madelyn about her mother dying and how terrible her childhood was…all the other stuff we read in that article."

Still not sure what Ty was telling him, Seth asked, "What's your point?"

"My point is I never got a chance to tell Madelyn what you and I discussed with Pete. As soon as we left there Saturday morning, I got called to Washington, D.C. I didn't get home until last night. And, frankly, Seth, explaining to Madelyn that you didn't want a nanny and that she should be helping you, not Lucy, wasn't my high priority after not seeing my fiancée for two days."

Seth laughed. "So tell her now."

Ty shook his head. "In the three days that have passed since Saturday, Captain Bunny apparently called out her personal militia to make sure Lucy's had enough help that you would forget all about the nanny. By now, Lucy's probably made friends with nearly every woman in Porter and they think you're the enemy."

"*I'm* the enemy!" Seth gasped, bolting up in his chair. "I'm trying to keep my son from a life of bodyguards and photo ops. These people should be helping *me!*"

"They would be if we could tell them the truth. But now

that they've sided with Lucy, the truth's not our friend. If we explain that you want custody, all they'll see is you taking a baby away from his mother—the sweet young woman they've gotten to know because they've been helping her."

Frustrated, Seth balled up a piece of paper and tossed it to a nearby trash can. "Great."

"Well, you weren't supposed to wrestle Owen away from Lucy anyway. You're supposed to demonstrate to Lucy that you're the best person to raise Owen through his childhood—away from the palace, bodyguards and even the current king. Did you read the article Pete gave you?"

Seth nodded. "Yeah, King Dad's a real piece of work. I can't imagine he would ever let Owen do anything normal. The kid probably really will be wearing purple tights and a velvet robe."

"Which only confirms what we already know. We've got to keep him here in Porter."

"Yeah, right. And how do we do that now that our plan has failed?"

"It hasn't failed. It just needs to be amended. Instead of showing Lucy you're a good dad, change the strategy to showing her *Porter* is a good place for a kid to grow up. And the beauty of this shift is that you can use the women who are coming and going as a way to demonstrate that Porter is a friendly, close-knit community. It isn't a big, lonely castle. It isn't a place where Owen will be photographed if he goes outside with a baseball and bat. If anybody watches Owen, it will be to make sure he isn't being stalked, pursued, or even observed. We've got a whole town full of people who would be surrogate bodyguards. And many of them are already Lucy's friends."

Seth smiled. "That's really good, Ty."

"Because it's the truth. You have the truth on your side, Seth, and you have to use it. If the nanny brigade wants to watch Owen, let them. Show Lucy this is what we do in Porter. When you go home this afternoon, if you find a gaggle of girls hovering over the baby, tell Lucy that while there are people to watch him, the two of you should go to the den and talk."

The thought of being alone in a room with Lucy—no baby for a buffer, no nanny brigade to run interference—froze the air in Seth's lungs. "You want me to be alone in a room with her?"

Ty eyed him suspiciously. "Is there some reason you shouldn't?"

"No!" Seth quickly denied. "It's just that…that…"

That he really had been playing with fire the day before. When he'd pulled Owen from Lucy's arms, he'd lingered beside her long enough to be sure she really was having reactions to him, but in doing that he'd also shown her he was still attracted to her. Then they'd had the conversation about her father keeping them apart, which meant they were no longer mutually disappointed in each other. So there was no ill will to assure that neither of them would act on the attraction that still pulsed between them. Seth might want to remind her she liked him, but he didn't think it was safe or smart for either of them to test their resistance.

He drew a quick breath and said, "Being alone to talk doesn't work because I'm not supposed to bring up visitation until I have a chance to show her I'm a normal guy."

Ty frowned as if he knew Seth was only telling him part of the truth, but he didn't press the issue. Instead, he said, "You're not going out of the room to talk as much as you're going out of the room to get Lucy accustomed to leaving Owen in the hands of the residents of Porter. You can talk about anything you want. But if I were you, I'd talk about what a great town Porter is and what great people we have. If there's somebody in your kitchen taking care of your son, that's not merely your perfect opportunity to talk to Lucy, it's also a real live demonstration of what you're saying. The people in this town look out for each other."

Seth breathed a sigh of relief that Ty might have honed in on the fact that Seth was still attracted to Lucy, but it appeared he wasn't going to mention it. Hopefully that was because Ty understood Seth might be attracted to his princess, but he knew better than to act on it. He'd once craved Lucy sexually so much that he'd convinced himself lust was love and had never considered the ramifications of being married to a princess. And that was really what had caused all the trouble. He'd let overwhelming sexual attraction fool him into forgetting reality. And reality was Lucy was a princess. If Seth got involved with her again, he would ultimately become part of her family…her *monarchy*. And he'd be the one wearing purple tights. Worse, Owen would then have no advocate because Seth would have joined the opposing side.

No way. He simply couldn't desert Owen like that.

"So you want me to use the nanny brigade to get time to talk to Lucy."

"Yes, so you can lay the groundwork about the great people who live in Porter. If she likes the town before you start your campaign to convince her that you're the best person to raise Owen, you'll have a much easier time."

Seth nodded. "Okay. When I go home today, I won't fight with the nanny brigade, I'll use them."

Ty beamed. "Exactly."

* * *

Though it was still morning, Seth decided to go home immediately to put Ty's plan into motion with Lucy and whatever neighbor he found at his kitchen table holding his son. Fortified in his resolve not to give in to the attraction that sizzled between him and Lucy, he also considered changing out of his sweatshirt and jeans before he encountered her. But after reminding himself that Owen's future was at stake, Seth was no longer concerned about a piddly sexual attraction. Owen was more important than a few hormones.

He stepped into the kitchen fully prepared to be the picture-perfect Porter resident, somebody who would raise Owen in a wonderful small town, but the room was empty. No Lucy. No nanny brigade.

"Lucy!" he called, walking from the kitchen into the corridor and then the foyer. "Luce! Where are you?"

When he didn't get an answer, he decided she was probably in the master bedroom, napping. Which meant Owen was probably sleeping, too. Of course, if he wasn't, if the baby had awakened and simply hadn't yet started screaming, this was a great opportunity for Seth to demonstrate that he could be good with the baby.

Taking the steps two at a time, Seth rushed to the second floor and down the hall to the master bedroom. He quietly eased the door open and stepped inside. The sheer drapes were drawn and the blinds were closed, darkening the room enough that it could have been midnight. Still, he could see enough to realize that Lucy wasn't on the bed. He took the few steps into the room and noticed that Owen was sleeping soundly in the bassinet.

Seth's heart expanded with love. His little boy only had

wisps of sandy brown hair and his feet didn't seem to reach the bottoms of his blue terry-cloth pajamas, but to Seth, Owen was perfect. He couldn't stem the flood of tenderness that swamped him and took a quick breath, letting the knowledge that he was a father seep into his soul. And, as always, that resulted in a surge of protectiveness that wouldn't allow him to stand by and do nothing while this tiny little boy was absorbed by an entire kingdom.

The bathroom door suddenly opened and Lucy stepped out, wearing a loosely belted robe. Her dark hair was wet, as if she'd washed it and only towel-dried it. Damp curls caressed her shoulders and led Seth's eyes to the V created where the two sides of her robe met. Because the garment wasn't secured, he could see the swell of her breasts.

Apparently having noticed the path of his gaze, Lucy quickly tightened her belt. "Is there something I can do for you?"

Seth took a step back. "I just came up to check on you. I saw Owen, and…" He stopped, angry that he had to explain himself but even more angry that she'd so quickly covered herself as if he were some kind of pervert. She knew better. He'd never touched her without her permission. She was perfectly safe with him.

He combed his fingers through his hair. "Look, Lucy. I recognize it's probably uncomfortable for you to have me in your room right now, but this was my bedroom first and coming in here was second nature. I didn't mean anything by it."

"I know."

Unfortunately, she tightened the belt again and righteous indignation shimmered through Seth. "What I'm saying is that you have nothing to worry about from me."

She drew a quick breath. "I'm not worried about you."

She might not be "worried" but Seth could see wariness in her eyes, but he suddenly realized she'd said, "I'm not worried about *you*," and recognized that had to mean she was worried about *herself* and her own reactions to him.

He squelched the urge to feel complimented. What Lucy was doing was being honest. And if she was having trouble handling things, then he had to show her he could be trustworthy enough for both of them. The wise thing to do would be to get them out of this bedroom. That was when he remembered Ty's plan.

"You know, while Owen's sleeping, this would be a good time for us to discuss a few things."

She stepped away, over to the vanity, where she grabbed a hairbrush and began pulling it through her abundant curls.

Mesmerized, Seth watched the brush glide from her temple to her shoulder and then back up again. She had wonderful thick, soft hair. The kind of hair a man could filter through his fingers simply for the pleasure of feeling its silkiness. In the four weeks they'd lived together, he'd done exactly that more times than he could count.

"Seth, by the time I'm dressed, Owen will be awake again."

Hypnotized by the strokes of the brush through her long locks, Seth hardly heard Lucy. He felt himself being drawn back in time. He remembered lying on the huge bed of Lucy's Miami apartment. With the evening sun saying goodbye by spreading a ray of hazy light across the bottom of her floral bedspread, and Lucy pressed against his side after making love, he would thread his fingers through her soft hair and they would talk. That was when he had told her about his dad. That was how he'd explained his relationship with Ty. That was also when he'd told her about Cooper.

"Besides, I need to dry this hair before it dries on its own and I'm left with nothing but a head full of fuzz."

Trapped in his memories, Seth stared at her, consumed by how much he had forgotten about their relationship.

Lucy sighed. Apparently thinking he hadn't replied because he didn't understand what she'd said, she added, "When naturally curly hair air-dries, you get fuzz, you don't get curls. It should be called naturally fuzzy hair, not naturally curly."

He took a quick breath and forced himself back into the conversation. "Yeah. If you say so."

"I say so. Let me dry my hair."

She'd said that before. Probably fifty times. After swimming. But more so giggling with glee after making love in the shower. Those crystal clear memories swept over Seth like a steamroller. Stealing his breath. He knew that if he'd allowed himself to remember any of these things before this, he could have minimized them, reduced them. Instead, undistorted and probably correct, his recollections had a powerful effect. He felt as if no time had passed since he'd held her, kissed her, walked hand in hand along the beach with her.

Knowing this trip down memory lane wasn't helping, Seth had to get out of the room. "Once you dry your hair, come downstairs and we'll talk."

"If Owen doesn't awaken."

"If Owen does wake up, I'll hold him while we talk."

With that, he left the room and headed down the back stairway to the kitchen. He half expected to see a middle-aged woman at his round oak table, but the room was still empty. Because it was a little after eleven, Seth pulled the deli meat and cheese from the refrigerator and scavenged for where the nanny brigade had hidden the rolls.

By the time he had sandwiches and coffee made, Lucy came into the room. Dressed in jeans that appeared to be three sizes too big and an equally large T-shirt, and holding Owen, she nonetheless looked absolutely beautiful to Seth. Still, that was the problem. He had to learn to be around her without noticing her beauty, without thinking of her in sexual terms. He had to see her as the mother of his son, the woman who would allow him to raise their little boy through his childhood if he could prove to her that he was trustworthy.

"I made some sandwiches for lunch."

She nodded and slowly, almost fearfully, walked to the round table and took a seat.

And the best way to prove he was trustworthy was to deal with the fact that everything had changed between them the day before. And the best way to deal with that was to face it head-on. "I'm not going to bite."

She almost smiled. "I know."

"And I'm really not the enemy," Seth said, pouring steaming coffee into the two mugs he'd placed on the table.

"It's better for Owen if we're not enemies."

"I agree," Seth said. This little meeting was exactly what they both needed. She couldn't be afraid of him. He couldn't spend the rest of his life lusting after her. Twenty minutes alone behaving like mature adults should completely solve this problem.

He sat on the chair across from her and reached for a sandwich. Silence descended. Seth swore he could hear the clock ticking. Desperately trying to think of something to say that would ease them toward a friendship, he said, "So, did Owen take a long nap this morning?"

She cleared her throat. "Sort of." She shrugged. "Longer than usual, anyway. I spent the first hour half expecting him to get up, waiting for his cry, lying on the bed."

The memory of her lying on her bed in Miami flashed into Seth's brain, but this time she was the one confiding things while he dressed for work. She hadn't really told him secrets because she laughed that her life was an open book. What she'd told him were her plans for her life. Though she was an architect, she couldn't actually pursue employment, but maintaining her father's vast real estate holdings was something of a career in itself. She oversaw all building, handled all renovations, met with contractors and even visited job sites. She'd worked so hard and was so independent that it was easy for Seth to forget she was royalty. And equally easy to understand why he had been floored that she'd run when her dad crooked his finger.

"I'm glad Owen slept," he replied slowly, cautiously, wishing he wasn't remembering how wonderfully normal she was, wishing he could think of her again as a stuffed shirt, weak-willed royal, so he could dislike her.

Particularly since Lucy clearly did not want to be friendly with him. Not meeting his eyes, she busied herself with getting a sandwich and sadness poured through Seth. He remembered days at the beach, dinners on the water, nights spent as close as two people could be and now she didn't even want to talk to him.

He took a quiet breath. "You look very natural with a baby."

She glanced over and in her eyes Seth saw the same sadness that had just filled his soul, proving she wasn't as impervious as she wanted him to believe. But before she could say anything, a knock sounded at the kitchen door. Without waiting to be admitted, Mildred walked in with two friends.

"This is Jeanie and Deb," she said, pointing at the two women behind her. Jeanie had red hair. Deb was a short and thin brunette. "We brought a little something for the baby," she said, nodding at the brightly wrapped packages held by the women.

Obviously relieved, Lucy said, "Oh, how nice!"

Though Ty believed Seth needed the women who had entered his kitchen, Seth was tired of never having two minutes to himself. Two minutes with Lucy. It seemed everybody on the planet had more say than he had about how much time he would spend with her. Still, he didn't dare go there. Especially not in front of the nanny brigade.

Focusing on the other thing that was beginning to dent his male pride, the fact that people kept bringing clothes for his child as if he were unable to support one measly baby, he pointed at the presents. "I can buy the things my son needs."

Mildred laughed and made her way to the coffeepot. "Oh, Seth, you are such a man. Don't you know that women don't buy presents for babies because we think the baby needs fifty-one rattles, twelve stuffed bears and a hundred sleepers? We buy presents because we like to shop for baby things. It's in our genes." She paused and turned to her friends. "You guys want coffee?"

Jeanie brightened. "No, but I wouldn't mind holding the baby."

"No, me first!" Deb said, walking over to Lucy who had risen from the table to join the women.

Seth looked over at Owen, who was nestled in the crook of Lucy's arm. Sound asleep, Seth's son had both fists bunched at his cheeks. His forehead was wrinkled like a basset hound's. His color was somewhere between red and purple. But he was Seth's flesh and blood, maybe the only child he would ever have, and he suddenly felt betrayed that his time, his first real personal time with his son and his son's mother, was being stolen from him.

Jeanie slipped Owen from Lucy's hands. "Oh, my God! He's beautiful."

Seth watched as Deb and Mildred crowded around Jeanie. Both sighed.

Lucy said, "I think he cooed this morning."

Mildred spun to face her. "You think he *said* something!"

"Just a goo or a coo…"

Mildred's face became soft and dreamy. "Sweetie, he's probably a genius. Seth and his brothers had always been bright—the top of their classes. So if there are any kind of brains at all in that royal family of yours, this kid is destined for greatness."

Lucy laughed. "I'm not sure of the IQ's in my family, but nearly everyone was educated at Oxford."

Impressed, all three female visitors said, "Ohhhh…"

Seth took a quiet breath. For someone who wouldn't say two words to him, Lucy was suddenly animated and happy. She couldn't have more clearly expressed her dislike for him if she'd actually said the words. And that feeling of betrayal he had…

Well, he suddenly realized that when he'd given Lucy her privacy to dress, she'd probably called Mildred.

He turned and left the room. If that wasn't proof Seth couldn't trust her, he didn't know what was.

Chapter Five

The following Monday morning, when Seth arrived at the Bryant Development building after a weekend of having absolutely no time alone with either Lucy or the baby, he saw Madelyn and Ty waiting at the front lobby elevator.

Walking toward them, Seth noticed that Ty wore an emerald-green sweater over a white oxford cloth shirt and dark trousers and he marveled again at what a difference Madelyn had made in his brother's life. In a way, by changing Ty Madelyn had altered the entire dynamic of their company. The dress code had been abolished, which relaxed the atmosphere enough that the employees started talking about things they'd never before dared discuss and now Bryant Development had a job-share option for working parents. And Ty was becoming beloved by his employees.

Ironically, as Ty's world got better, more comfortable, more relaxed, Seth's got more and more confusing. With women who seemed to come and go from his home at whim, keeping him from the woman he needed to convince he could be a good dad and also keeping him from the baby he wanted to raise, Seth's world tumbled further and further toward complete chaos.

"Hey, Dad," Madelyn said, greeting Seth as he walked up to them. Like Ty, Madelyn had dressed in slacks and a simple yellow sweater that complemented her red hair. The elevator doors opened and they stepped inside.

"How was your weekend?" Madelyn asked as the car began to climb.

"Fine," Seth mumbled.

Obviously hearing his lack of enthusiasm, Madelyn studied his face. Seth knew she undoubtedly noticed his ragged appearance, but, luckily, her office was on the second floor and the bell for that stop rang before she could question him.

She stood on tiptoes and kissed Ty's cheek, then bounded out. "See you at lunch," she called with a wave.

"Yeah, I'll see you at lunch," Ty agreed, waving as she turned to walk down the hall. But when the door closed behind her, Ty spun to face Seth and said, "You look like hell. What's going on?"

"Nothing."

Ty's eyes narrowed. "Nothing?"

"The nannies are coming in pairs now. Somebody to watch the baby, somebody to occupy Lucy. I'm starting to think there's a conspiracy to keep me away from both Lucy and the baby."

As the elevator doors swung open on the top floor, Ty said, "There may be." He caught Seth's sleeve, preventing him from turning to the right to go to his office. "But let's not talk about it here. Come with me to my office."

They walked in silence to Ty's office suite where Ty's secretary, Joni, an older brunette with three kids—all of whom were fast approaching their teens—greeted them. "Good morning, guys."

"Morning, Joni," Ty said absently. He grabbed his messages and walked past her desk.

Seth said, "Good morning, Joni," then followed his older brother into his office and waited while Ty closed the door.

"So what's going on?"

"Some days I don't even get to *see* Owen," Seth said, suddenly abundantly annoyed. His anger wasn't simply caused by his inability to prove himself to Lucy. He had a son, damn it, and he hardly got to see the kid!

"This might be working to your advantage, Seth," Ty said as he fell into his tall-back office chair.

"I know. I know. As long as Lucy is depending upon your future mother-in-law's friends for help, she's getting to know the townspeople."

"And she's growing to like them."

"Probably. The only person she doesn't seem to like is me."

"So, don't worry about it. Once she likes the town, she'll begin seeing you in a different light and she'll like you."

Right.

"In fact, I think I have a way to speed up the process."

Positive anything would be an improvement, Seth said, "What's your idea?"

"Well, we want Lucy to like and trust the people of this town."

"Right."

"And the only time she seems to be uncomfortable is when you're around."

"Thanks."

Ty laughed. "Seth, it's nothing personal."

Right. Easy for Ty to say. "So what's your idea?"

"We don't know how long Lucy plans to stay, but if I were to send you out of town every week for the next few weeks, she might stay longer. She would also have a couple of five-day blocks to get accustomed to your house, your neighbors, our town, without the reminder of why she shouldn't like it here."

Seth gaped at his older brother. "Gee, thanks, Ty."

"You know what I mean. She's only been here a little over a week. So it's natural that she's uncomfortable. If we remove you from the picture a couple of times, then she'll have less to be nervous about and adjust more quickly. Once she adjusts to your house and the town, it's a short step to her being comfortable around you. And pretty soon, the whole picture will have fallen into place."

It wasn't a perfect plan, but, unfortunately, after the last disastrous encounter he'd had with Lucy that had caused her to double up on visitors to avoid being alone with him, Seth knew Ty had a valid point. If Seth were to get custody of Owen, it would be because Lucy believed Owen would be safe in Porter. It would be because Lucy believed Owen could have a normal childhood in Porter. It would be because Lucy liked Porter. And as far as Seth could tell, Ty was right. The one thing holding her back from really liking the town was him. He might as well step aside and let Porter strut its stuff.

"Great. Send me away."

The following afternoon, after a plane ride that took about forty minutes and a bumpy SUV journey that felt like a lifetime, Seth found himself in a town so far in the wilds that they didn't have cell phone reception. He checked into a hotel where he shared the bathroom with three other guests, then went in search of the county engineer who would have the specifics on the project Ty wanted to bid. Tuesday through Friday, the only contact Seth had with anyone from Porter was the call he made to Ty from a pay phone in the general store. By Friday night, he was so eager to get home he nearly danced with joy. But, of course, he couldn't get a flight out until Saturday morning.

He arrived in Porter late Saturday afternoon to find Lucy not only happy and energetic, but also looking more like the woman he had met in Miami. The first week Lucy had lived in his home, Seth had been so preoccupied with the baby that he hadn't really noticed Lucy was still swollen from her pregnancy. But after a week away, and two weeks since she'd had the baby, it was clear that she had dropped most of the weight that she had gained. And she looked really good.

Standing by the kitchen counter, far enough away that Seth knew Lucy couldn't see him, he found himself mesmerized by her and stopped his staring. Lord knew he didn't want to scare her into bringing in three members of the brigade.

But when he realized no one was paying any attention to him—Lucy and Mildred were at the kitchen table talking about Owen—he let his gaze tiptoe over to Lucy again and he drank in every bit of her physical perfection. Her shiny hair. Her pink cheeks. The fabulous curve of her waist. When he remembered the way that curve felt against his palm, he knew he'd let his casual glance go a little too far, and he forced his attention on the conversation at the table between Lucy and Mildred.

"Since Seth is going out of town again this week," Mildred said as she set her coffee mug on the table, "I'll ask Audrey and Penney if they want to come over again Tuesday and Thursday nights like we did last week. In fact, if Seth's going to be out of town a lot, we should form a card club that would meet those same nights at your house so you don't have to take Owen outside."

"That's a great idea!" Lucy said, and from the way her eyes lit, Seth knew Ty had been correct. Because Seth was away, Lucy was getting to know the people of Porter in a way she couldn't when he was home. And she was growing to like them. They even referred to Seth's house as her house.

On Sunday when Lucy told Seth that she had spoken with her dad and decided to stay in Arkansas a little longer, it was clear Ty's plan was working. Seth mentioned his surprise that the king wasn't rushing to see Xavier's future ruler, but Lucy casually explained that the country's legislature was in session and her father couldn't get away.

Seth might buy into the story that King Alfredo couldn't get away to come to Arkansas, but he suddenly wondered why the king hadn't demanded Lucy return home with Xavier Island's future king. On the heels of that, he realized no reporter had ever approached him about either his marriage or Lucy's pregnancy, and the whole scheme fell into place. Seth would bet his last dollar that King Alfredo hadn't allowed Lucy to stay in Miami to finish his mansion but, instead, to keep her hasty marriage and her pregnancy a secret.

Which meant if Lucy returned to Xavier Island with a baby, the shocked media would investigate and any hope the king had of sanitizing the story of Lucy's marriage and Owen's conception would go out the window.

Whatever the king's motive, Seth knew the situation worked to his advantage because Lucy was becoming very happy in Porter. So on Monday he dutifully ventured off to Pleasure, Utah, and the Monday after that he boarded a plane for Iowa.

The Iowa trip wasn't part of Ty's efforts to get Seth out of Lucy's hair. It had been scheduled for months, so Seth couldn't complain that he was getting tired of traveling or remind Ty that Owen was growing up without him. Besides, everything was evolving perfectly. Lucy seemed to thrive in the time Seth was away. So, fine. Seth would rumble around the country and give her free run of his house, and time to make friends with the neighbors and get her gorgeous figure and energy back.

He spent that week with negotiators for the unions representing the laborers in the area where Ty intended to build a huge office complex. After five days of nothing but cigar smoke and talk about wages and benefits, Seth was ready to go home, but Ty called and insisted that this weekend was the worst time for Seth to invade their space. The girls were having some kind of party for Lucy. Not exactly a baby shower, since they'd already bought enough gifts, but more of a girl-talk session where everybody got a chance to see Owen and all of his baby pictures.

Instead of going home that Friday night, Seth was shipped to Idaho to look at land. There, at least, Seth had cell phone service—if he stood in the right spot.

"So how's it going?" he asked Lucy when he called home the following Wednesday. He'd spent nearly four weeks on the road. Owen was now five weeks old and Seth's neighbors knew more about his son than he did. Plus, Seth might not know much about the length of Xavier Island's legislative session, but he sensed his time with Owen and Lucy was running out. Any day now, her father could show up. Since he hadn't gone home the previous weekend, he didn't think a phone call was out of line.

He could picture Lucy's smile when she said, "Great! You should see Owen, Seth…"

Seth squeezed his eyes shut. He longed to see his son but more than that it sounded so good to hear Lucy say his name. To have her speak to him normally. To not be afraid or wary.

"He doesn't really talk, but he desperately wants to make sounds."

"How could you know that he *wants* to make sounds?" Seth asked with a laugh.

"I coo at him and he tries to mimic me. His little mouth moves like crazy, but nothing comes out. It's the sweetest thing," she said with a dreamy sigh.

Seth swallowed as three different varieties of appreciation tumbled through him. Appreciation for how well Lucy cared for Owen. Appreciation for how quickly she was catching on. Appreciation for how sweet her interactions with their baby seemed to be.

He tried to fight them but absolutely couldn't. Not when he was already overwhelmed with loneliness. Luckily, though, after the swell of appreciation came a sort of friendly feeling. They had missed this part of dating. They might have talked, but they had never just "been friends." Being friends with her, even getting to talk to her, was like water to a thirsty man.

When Lucy asked, "So what are you doing out there," Seth realized that she could be feeling the same thing he was. A desire to be friends. He perked up, thinking Ty's plan really was working. Lucy didn't hate him anymore!

"What am I doing right now?" Seth asked, glancing around at the quiet, all-but-deserted town. "Ty wants to bid on some road work. I'm evaluating the location."

"Really? As half owner of the company, you still go out and do the preliminary legwork?"

Not wanting to tell her they were making work for him to get him out of her hair, Seth said, "I'm not half owner. There are three of us who own this company."

"That's right. You have a brother."

"Yeah. Cooper."

"Did you guys ever find him?" Lucy asked innocently and Seth drew a quick breath, realizing again that he'd told Lucy much, much more about himself and his life than he thought he had.

Still, it was good to have something to talk about, something personal—but not something directly related to their relationship—that could bridge the gap that yawned between them. "I only recently convinced Ty that we should look for him in earnest."

"That's great."

"Yeah, it is," Seth agreed, suddenly buoyed. It felt good to talk about Cooper. Actually, it felt good to talk about anything familiar. He hadn't been around anyone he knew in weeks. But even when he was in Porter, Ty didn't talk as much as he once had, now that he had Madelyn in his life. And nearly everybody else in town worked for Bryant Development. So, the Bryants weren't much for airing personal business in town. Plus, Seth had apparently already told her a good bit about his life when they were together. He could talk about anything he wanted.

"Ty's changed a lot in the past few months."

"He seems very happy."

"He's ecstatic and that makes all of our lives better."
Lucy laughed.

Seth leaned against the rough wood of a porch brace in
front of a convenience store, pleased that he had amused her.
"Did you know the employees used to call him Tyrant Ty?"

"Oh, yeah," Lucy said with a giggle. "He scared the
pants off fifty percent of the crew you guys had working
on my dad's mansion before…before…"

"Before your dad fired us," Seth said easily, as if it were
no big deal, so that part of their lives could come out in the
open and neither one of them would have to avoid it anymore. Then he quickly changed the subject. "So what else
has Owen done?"

"Not much. He likes to eat and sleep and watch me."

"So you two just stare at each other all day?"

She laughed again. "No! I set him in his bouncy chair
and secure it wherever I'm puttering and he watches me
do dishes or dust."

The thought of Princess Lucy doing dishes, dusting and
basically keeping his house livable sent a shaft of fear
through Seth. He was supposed to be keeping her comfortable and happy! Not treating her like hired help. Now that
he wasn't home, he should have brought his maid back.

"Lucy, I have someone who comes in to do that stuff. I
gave her a paid leave when you first arrived so you would
have your privacy," he lied, but he decided he didn't have
a choice. "So if you'd like her back, I would be happy to…"

"No!" Lucy gasped. "My gosh, Seth, everything's perfect. In fact," her voice dipped and Seth had to strain to hear
her, "I want to thank you for letting me stay here."

And for leaving, Seth thought, as his chest tightened
with both gladness that he'd done something nice for her

and sorrow that she really didn't like him. But he didn't say anything. The life of the mother of his child was absolutely perfect. No matter that his not being around was part of that perfection. No matter that they'd spent every minute of every day together for four wonderful weeks. Times had changed. She was happier when he wasn't around.

"Hey, look, I gotta go. I'm in front of the convenience store," he said, making the place sound busy as he glanced inside at the empty aisles and the clerk who napped behind the cash register. "I need to get out of everybody's way."

"Okay, Seth. I'll see you this weekend."

"Yeah, I'll see you this weekend," he agreed and quickly hung up the phone. He couldn't stay on the phone while his lungs were tight with missing her and his gut twisted with the knowledge that her life was so much better without him. In fact, he wasn't really sure how he would manage spending the weekend at the house when he knew how much happier she was when he wasn't there.

But he needn't have worried. Friday afternoon, Ty hunted Seth down and explained that a crisis had arisen and Seth couldn't go home that weekend, either. He had to go to Arizona. Seth hopped a plane, then a commuter, then rented a car and drove to another remote site. He met the foreman who outlined the impending crisis Ty discussed, but Seth looked at the blueprints in front of him and easily pointed out the solution. The foreman, nodded, pleased that Seth had found his answer, but Seth had the feeling he had been set up.

When he found himself alone in his hotel room that night, with nothing to do and nothing really on his agenda because the "problem" had been solved, he *knew* he had been set up.

By the following Thursday, in spite of his now daily calls to Lucy, Seth had had it. Ty was making up trouble that was insulting Seth's intelligence. Lucy was doing fine without him. Six-week-old Owen was growing by leaps and bounds. Seth's son had had his second pediatrician appointment. He'd gotten a tour of the town from Madelyn. The ladies at church had bought him enough clothes for six kids. If Seth didn't soon go home, they'd have Owen enrolled in kindergarten.

He called an airline and growled for the entire two-hour drive to the airport. Blasted Rocky Mountains! Blasted Ty! No, stupid, stupid *Seth* for listening to anyone other than himself. Sure, he agreed that Lucy needed some time alone to discover the town and to make friends with the towns-people. Great. He could handle that. And, yes, Seth rec-ognized that he was the biggest cause of her initial anxiety. But he'd been talking with Lucy and he knew she was fine. Sometimes, he even suspected she enjoyed getting his calls.

So he was going the hell home!

When he stepped into his front entryway, it was two o'clock in the morning. He was tired. His feet throbbed. His back ached.

And Owen was screaming.

He kicked off his loafers, bounded up the steps and burst into the master bedroom where he found Lucy walk-ing the floor with a bundle of baby who absolutely refused to quiet down.

"Please, Owen," she said, sounding helpless. "I wish I knew what was wrong, but you can't tell me and I don't know what to do."

From behind her, Seth said, "Let me take him."

She whirled around. "Seth!"

He reached for sobbing Owen and cuddled the little boy against his chest. Ripple upon ripple upon ripple of emotion flooded through him. He was home. He was holding his son. Lucy needed him.

He let himself soak in and savor every tiny nuance of emotion as Owen quieted on his shoulder, before he said, "Lucy, what's going on here?"

She collapsed on the bed. "I'm sorry, Seth. I'm not the perfect mother I've been trying to lead you to believe I am. This whole time, friends of Penney Gentry have been helping me with Owen. I tricked you."

"You tricked me?"

"But I had good reason. I didn't want a nanny but more than that, I needed to learn how to care for Owen in the little bit of time I knew my dad would be unable to come after me. Penney Gentry and her friends agreed to teach me."

Seth sat beside her on the bed. Owen settled into Seth's shoulder, sniffling himself to sleep. "You weren't keeping me away because you don't like me?"

She blinked up at him. "What?"

"You just seemed so much happier without me that I…" Seth stopped. He hadn't kept himself away. Ty had helped. Still, Seth was an adult. He wasn't about to blame Ty for his own stupidity. So he might as well tell Lucy the whole truth.

"I stayed away because you seemed so much happier without me. And I wanted you to be happy and see what a great town Porter is so I would have at least a leg to stand on when you and I sat down to talk about…" He almost said *custody,* but knew he couldn't broach that until the time was right. So in the final seconds he said, "Visitation."

"Oh, Seth, I'm not going to lie to you. You're not going to get much time with Owen and when you do get to see him, you'll probably have to come to Xavier Island. As Xavier's future king, Owen will have to submit to my dad's authority more than any of my dad's other grandchildren will. But I promise to do my best to get you every minute I can. I'm on your side."

Because his plan was to convince her to let him have custody and he wasn't anywhere near ready to do that yet, he didn't protest what she'd said. In fact, he decided to pretend he hadn't heard it and focus on the positive.

"Then I'm on your side."

She drew a quick breath. "Thanks. I just couldn't refuse Penney and Mildred's help with the baby. I'd spent more time with nannies than with my mother when she died and her memory faded very quickly. I hardly missed her after only a few weeks because I hardly knew her. I don't want that to happen with Owen."

When Seth glanced down at Lucy, he saw the sheen of tears on her eyelashes. Shifting Owen so that he needed only one hand to secure his son against his shoulder, Seth reached down and lifted Lucy's chin so that he could look into her eyes. Guilt threaded through him because he intended to take Owen from her. But in the final analysis, if Owen lived with Seth, Lucy could easily visit Porter and Seth would also gladly let her take their son anytime she wanted as long as it didn't interfere with school. But if Owen lived in a castle on an island across the Atlantic, Seth wouldn't have the same option. Lucy had already admitted Seth would only see his son a few times a year—and then only on Xavier Island.

More than that, though, if Seth didn't get custody from Lucy, Owen wouldn't have a normal childhood.

But, again, this wasn't the time to mention all that. This

was the time for them to take their first real steps toward a friendship. "Then we'll make sure your son knows you."

She smiled and nodded. "Thanks."

Silence entered the room and for the first time since Owen had been born, Seth saw the exhaustion in Lucy's pretty brown eyes. Obviously she wasn't accepting help with Owen at night and Seth felt horrible for deserting her. He felt worse for not talking to her honestly before this.

"You look awful."

Lucy laughed. "Thanks, Seth. That's just what a woman wants to hear."

"I didn't mean it like it sounded. I said it because I shouldn't have deserted you since it's pretty clear the nanny brigade doesn't spend the night."

"Nanny brigade?" Lucy said, then laughed. "That's what you call Penney and her friends?"

"If you think about it, that's what they are."

"Yeah. I guess so. But I didn't let them help me at night because I don't want to become entirely dependent on them. I want to be Owen's mom."

The way she said it overwhelmed Seth with emotion. Having lived without parents from the time he was fifteen, it wasn't simply gratifying to his male ego that the mother of his child wanted to be a real mother. It was a blessing to know his son wouldn't suffer the fate he had. God willing, Owen would have the love and support of two parents for most of his life.

Overcome with gratitude, Seth didn't stop to think about consequences and bent his head and kissed her. When his mouth met the softness of her lips, his eyes closed in sweet appreciation. Memories overloaded his mind. Instincts surged to life. He combed the fingers of his free hand through her hair, and a thousand sensations thundered through him, the most potent of which was the desire to make love. But strangely, that instinct was the one that brought him to his senses.

They couldn't make love. They really shouldn't even be kissing. He needed her to like and trust him because he wanted his son. And if they took this relationship back to the sexual level, when there was no future for them, she would never trust him. Hell, he wouldn't trust himself.

He pulled away. For several seconds, he stared into her desire-glazed eyes, assuming from the fact that she didn't argue when he stopped and didn't do anything to encourage him to kiss her again that she had concluded the same things he had. They couldn't go back to their past and they didn't have a future.

Except as Owen's parents.

With Owen sleeping soundly on his shoulder, Seth rose from the bed and walked to the door. He would care for Owen tonight while she slept.

"Go to sleep."

Chapter Six

Though Owen's crying awakened Lucy the next morning, a flood of joy enveloped her when she opened her eyes. Seth had kissed her the night before! She rolled out of bed to get her hungry son, unable to stop the flow of happiness that poured through her.

But lifting Owen from his crib, she reminded herself that being joyful over that kiss wasn't necessarily good. She might be happy that Seth had kissed her, but she was also smart enough to know she shouldn't make too much of it. First, the circumstances in which he had kissed her had been charged with emotion. Second, the kiss had sealed a bond of sorts. The soft, sweet joining of their mouths hadn't been an expression of love as much as a commitment to work together.

That was the way she needed to view it. They'd been honest with each other for the first time since her arrival at his house and they'd formed a team of sorts. The kiss

An Important Message from the Editors

Dear Reader,

If you'd enjoy reading novels about rediscovery and reconnection with what's important in women's lives, then let us send you two free Harlequin® Next™ novels. These books celebrate the "next" stage of a woman's life because there's a whole new world after marriage and motherhood.

By the way, you'll also get a surprise gift with your two free books! Please enjoy the free books and gift with our compliments...

Pam Powers

Peel off Seal and Place Inside...

EDITOR'S FREE GIFT SEAL THANK YOU

We'd like to send you two free books to introduce you to our brand-new series – Harlequin® NEXT™! These novels by acclaimed award-winning authors are filled with stories about rediscovery and reconnection with what's important in women's lives. These are relationship novels about women redefining their dreams.

THERE'S THE LIFE YOU PLANNED. AND THERE'S WHAT COMES NEXT.

Your two books have a combined cover price of $11.00 in the U.S. and $13.00 in Canada, but are yours **FREE!** We'll even send you a wonderful surprise gift. You can't lose!

FREE BONUS GIFT!

We'll send you a wonderful surprise gift, absolutely FREE, just for giving Harlequin NEXT books a try! Don't miss out — **MAIL THE REPLY CARD TODAY!**

Order online at
www.TryNextNovels.com

THE EDITOR'S "THANK YOU" FREE GIFTS INCLUDE:

▶ Two BRAND-NEW Harlequin® Next™ Novels

▶ An exciting surprise gift

YES! I have placed my Editor's "thank you" Free Gifts seal in the space provided at right. Please send me 2 FREE books, and my FREE Mystery Gift. I understand that I am under no obligation to purchase anything further, as explained on the back and opposite page.

PLACE
FREE GIFTS
SEAL
HERE

356 HDL D72K   156 HDL D73J

FIRST NAME   LAST NAME

ADDRESS

APT.#   CITY

STATE/PROV.   ZIP/POSTAL CODE

Thank You!

(HN-TL-11/05)

The Reader Service — Here's How It Works:

Accepting your 2 free books and gift places you under no obligation to buy anything. You may keep the books and gift and return the shipping statement marked "cancel." If you do not cancel, about a month later we'll send you 3 additional books and bill you just $3.99 each in the U.S., or $4.74 each in Canada, plus 25¢ shipping & handling per book and applicable taxes if any.* That's the complete price and — compared to cover prices of $5.50 each in the U.S. and $6.50 each in Canada — it's quite a bargain! You may cancel at any time, but if you choose to continue, every month we'll send you 3 more books, which you may either purchase at the discount price or return to us and cancel your subscription.

*Terms and prices subject to change without notice. Sales tax applicable in N.Y. Canadian residents will be charged applicable provincial taxes and GST.

If offer card is missing write to: The Reader Service, 3010 Walden Ave., P.O. Box 1867, Buffalo, NY 14240-1867

BUSINESS REPLY MAIL
FIRST-CLASS MAIL   PERMIT NO. 717-003   BUFFALO, NY

POSTAGE WILL BE PAID BY ADDRESSEE

THE READER SERVICE
3010 WALDEN AVE
PO BOX 1867
BUFFALO NY 14240-9952

NO POSTAGE
NECESSARY
IF MAILED
IN THE
UNITED STATES

had been merely a way to seal their deal. They weren't about to get involved again. Otherwise, he would have taken the kiss further, deepened it, made it one of the passionate, romantic kisses they had shared when they'd thought they had a future. But he hadn't. He had said goodnight and run out of the bedroom.

If she thought he'd meant anything but a sealing of their commitment, Seth could break her heart. But more than that, *she* would be foolish to consider getting involved again. Seth may not have dumped her, but he hated her country and the monarchy to which she belonged. She had to remember that.

After changing Owen, Lucy took him downstairs to get a bottle. When she reached the back steps to the kitchen, she smelled the tantalizing aroma of bacon and knew Seth had awakened before her and was already making good on their agreement to work together.

Stepping off the bottom step, she said, "Good morning."

He turned from the stove, spatula in hand and smiled at her. Obviously not wanting to fry bacon in a suit and tie, Seth hadn't yet dressed for work but wore jeans and a sweatshirt. His short sandy brown hair was sexily tousled. His eyelids still drooped from need of sleep. But even the most handsome European prince had never looked as good to her as Seth looked right now.

Lucy's heart stumbled in her chest. The kiss they'd shared the night before came back in vivid detail in her mind, and she realized something important. With the desire that always simmered between them, it was surprising that they'd shared such a simple kiss. Even the day they'd met, they hadn't had a first kiss filled with expectancy and emotion. They'd shared a lust kiss. Every subsequent kiss they'd shared had been a promise of passion to come or an expression of passion.

But last night's kiss had been filled with expectancy and emotion. In that soft meeting of mouths that didn't make assumptions or push for things that couldn't be, Seth had told her that he liked her.

As she came to that conclusion, Lucy's heart once again stuttered. She'd loved making love with Seth, but all along she'd wanted him to like her. Now he did.

Still, it didn't matter. They didn't have a future. They needed to live separate lives.

"I made breakfast."

Trying to get her bearings and pretending everything could be normal between them, Lucy smiled and carried Owen to the refrigerator where she removed a bottle and put it in a warmer. "Did Owen wake you?"

"No, I set my alarm. It occurred to me last night that we were more or less counting on Owen to tell us what to do by crying. We'd never set a schedule or tried to beat him to the punch on anything."

"It's a good idea in theory, but so far Owen hasn't responded to our attempts to get him on a schedule," Lucy said, almost breathing a sigh of relief that everything between them really could be normal. She extracted the bottle from the warmer and walked to the table with Owen, who seemed comfortable with the quiet interaction of his parents.

"So Penney and her friends are really teaching you?"

"A lot! These women aren't merely bright. They're crafty. To them, mothering and creating a home are an art. And they know things about babies and houses that you won't find in any book."

Seth chuckled, returning his attention to the bacon he was frying. "I don't doubt that."

"It's going to be weird to tell them that I don't need them anymore."

Seth faced her again. "Why wouldn't you need them?"

Lucy shrugged. "Last night, we made a deal to work together. I didn't think that included outsiders."

"Can you handle Owen without them?"

"I can do all the day-to-day things with Owen on my own." She peeked over and caught Seth's gaze. "But I like their company and I like hearing their stories and I like knowing that if something comes up, any one of them is just a phone call away."

"Then let them come over."

"You're sure?"

Seth shrugged. "Those women are the most likely candidates to help me when I'm alone with Owen. We don't want to scare them off now."

Confused, because last night she had told Seth his visits with Owen would take place in the palace on Xavier Island, Lucy studied him. She'd wondered why he hadn't reacted the night before but now she knew he hadn't heard what she'd said, or if he had, he'd missed the part about visiting Owen at the palace.

Whatever the explanation, it was clear Seth hadn't fully understood what she told him. She debated outlining the situation again as Owen sucked greedily in the silence.

Seth brought bacon and toast to the table. "I hope this is a big enough breakfast."

"This is great," Lucy said, reaching with her free hand to pour a glass of orange juice from the carafe already on the table, as a new kind of tension snaked through her.

Nothing was ever simple or easy for her and Seth. They had sexual chemistry that could set the world on fire, but had to ignore it because they didn't fit into each other's lives. They shared a son, but couldn't raise him together. Now she had to explain to Seth that he couldn't even have normal visitation with his son, because Owen Bryant would someday be a king.

It was no wonder Seth hated their monarchy.

Seth brought the coffeepot to the table and said, "Can I pour you a cup?"

With guilt poking at her like nails, Lucy said, "I'll get some later."

Seth sat on the chair across from her and made a sandwich with the buttered toast and bacon. "We might as well decide a few things right now."

Knowing she couldn't live with this guilt, which meant she couldn't put off making sure Seth understood his limited visitation rights, Lucy took a quick breath, ready to jump into her explanation, but Seth spoke before she got the chance.

"Since Owen seems to wake at five-thirty, we'll set our alarms for five. We'll get up before him and more or less be ready for him."

"As soon as Owen hears my alarm go off," Lucy reminded Seth, "he'll get up."

"Okay, how about this? I'll set *my* alarm for five-fifteen, get up and get a bottle warmed. Then we'll let him sleep until five-thirty when we'll wake him."

"We'll wake him?" Lucy asked, wide-eyed.

"We're putting him on a schedule, remember?"

"I don't know. I told you, Seth, we already tried to get him on a schedule and it didn't work," Lucy said, not wanting to argue with Seth, who was only trying to be a good dad and who already got so very little say in raising his son. But she also saw any chance that she might get a few extra minutes of precious sleep slipping away.

The kitchen door opened and Audrey walked in. Her eyes widened when she saw Seth. "Seth! I didn't know you were here."

"It's okay," Seth said, motioning her inside. "I know all about you and how you've been helping Lucy. In fact, I appreciate it. Want some coffee?"

Audrey shrugged out of her sweater. "Just juice," she said and ambled over to the cupboard. Glass in hand, she grinned at Lucy. "Because I'm pregnant!"

Lucy gasped. Seth turned around in his chair. "Really?"

Audrey laughed. "Yes, but keep it a secret."

"Okay," Seth said, motioning for her to join them at the table. "We were just discussing setting our alarms to get up before Owen and creating a routine for him," he said as Audrey took her seat and reached for the carafe of juice. "What do you think?"

"Mildred's tried and it failed."

"I still want to try again." Seth turned to Lucy. "We'll talk about it when I get home."

Lucy said, "Okay."

Seth rose from his chair. "I'm going to get dressed for work now, but I'll be down to say goodbye to Owen before I leave."

He turned and walked to the back stairway. Lucy and Audrey stared at the wall that hid the steps, listening to Seth's footfalls and waiting for the sound of his bedroom door to close before Audrey said, "You two talked?"

"Yeah. He came in last night when I couldn't get Owen to sleep."

"Was it ugly?"

She shook her head, struggling to hide a smile that arose at the memory. For as much as she knew they had no future, she still treasured every interaction she had with Seth. "No. He was very understanding. I don't know how I could have forgotten that about him."

"Maybe because you only knew him a few weeks?" Audrey suggested with a laugh.

Lucy shook her head. "I might have only known him a few weeks, but we were together twenty-four hours a day. First at work, then at my apartment. I saw the way he treated his employees. I knew he was a patient man with a good sense of humor. Now that I'm remembering all that, I'm embarrassed that I wasn't honest with him in the first place."

"I think your nanny argument got in the way of either of you seeing clearly."

Lucy nodded. "I guess."

"It'll be better this way."

Lucy nodded again.

Audrey grinned. "We'll be like one big, happy family."

One more time, Lucy smiled and nodded. But inside she was feeling all kinds of crazy things. She'd forgotten so many things about their relationship and incorrectly remembered so many others that she had to wonder if she wasn't wrong about other things, too—such as his feeling about being married to a royal. Her dad had set it up so she believed that Seth had changed his mind about being married to a royal, but Seth had never really said that. Sure, he hadn't appreciated her running home when her dad had summoned her, but that was as much as she knew about how he felt because they hadn't seen each other. So was she jumping to another conclusion when she assumed Seth didn't want to be married to a royal?

She stopped her thoughts. Seth was a straightforward, bold guy. If he wanted her back, he would seduce her. The memory of just how easily he could seduce her tightened her chest and filled her with tingles until she remembered the kiss from the night before. If Seth wanted her, he could have had her. But he never took the kiss beyond the bounds of propriety.

In fact, now that she thought about it, Seth's kiss from the night before was actually proof that he *didn't* want her.

So she had to stop thinking as if he did.

Seth arrived at the Bryant Building ready to get back to work if only because being busy would keep him from thinking about Lucy and the impossibility of their situation.

But he also knew Ty would be angry that Seth had returned from out of town early. So he spent the morning more or less hiding, analyzing materials reports from the estimating department. When Ty's secretary, Joni, called to schedule lunch that day for Seth and Ty, Seth agreed. It was better to face the music over food.

At eleven-thirty, he met his brother in the parking lot by Ty's black SUV and for the next ten minutes sat in silence as they drove to the diner on Main Street.

Ty waited until they had settled in a rear booth before he said, "So are you going to tell me why you're back two days early?"

Seth didn't hesitate. "I have a son. I have to convince Lucy to let me raise Owen in Porter. I can't do that in God-Knows-Where, U.S.A. Besides, Lucy and I talked last night. The games are over."

"Good."

"Good?" Seth asked, totally confused. "You sent me away for five long weeks. Lucy's been learning to care for Owen that whole time. One of these days, her dad is going to just arrive and take her and Owen back to Xavier Island, and she and I will have nothing settled."

"Except that you respect each other."

Seth looked at Ty over his coffee cup as an ugly suspicion formed. "You *planned* this?"

Ty sighed. "No, Seth. I didn't. I think the result you got was a happy accident. The way Penney told Madelyn the story this morning, if Owen hadn't been screaming last night when you got home, you and Lucy probably wouldn't have talked and you wouldn't have formed your team."

Seth set his cup on the table. "Talk about a gossip network. Penney wasn't even the one at the house this morning. Audrey was. What do these women do, issue press releases?"

"I'm guessing it had more to do with e-mail. If our construction teams were half as efficient at communicating as these women are, our projects would never hit a snag."

They were quiet for a minute and eventually Seth said, "So you think it's good that Lucy and I more or less formed a team?"

"You don't?"

"I do, but you just seem…"

…to have switched sides, Seth thought, but he didn't say it. Instead, he paused, remembering how Ty's plan had gone from keeping Seth out of town for blocks of time to keeping Seth away even over weekends. He knew his older brother didn't do anything on a whim. Something had happened to make him believe that Seth being away all the

time would somehow force him and Lucy to talk. But why would he want Seth and Lucy to talk when his original plan had been to keep them apart?

Suddenly he knew.

"You've spent time with Lucy, haven't you?"

Ty sighed. "Madelyn and I would have been rude not to visit while you were away."

Seth gaped at his brother as his suspicions were confirmed. "You're on her side!"

"I wouldn't say I'm on her side because there are no sides. This is about Owen, doing the best thing for Owen and the best thing for Owen is to have him raised in Porter." Ty paused and sighed again. "But we also like Lucy a great deal. She and Madelyn are becoming good friends. When we visited while you were away, I started to feel horrible that we intend to take her baby away from her. Pretty soon, I began to think that wasn't the right thing to do at all."

Angry that Ty had turned traitor, but not about to say anything until he was sure he had heard everything Ty had to say, Seth leaned back on the booth. "Really."

"Madelyn and I think that maybe the two of you acted hastily in getting a divorce."

"We didn't get a divorce. Our marriage wasn't valid in the first place because Lucy was betrothed to someone else."

"And now she's not betrothed anymore. Because she got pregnant by someone other than the prince she was supposed to marry, the betrothal was terminated. The road is clear for you, Seth. You could remarry this woman tomorrow."

Seth only stared at his older brother. "Are you kidding me?"

"No, think this through. If you marry her, there's no custody or visitation to work out."

"In the first place, who says she would marry me? In the second, I wouldn't remarry her on a lost bet! I might like her…" *Really like her. Really miss her. Really enjoy having her around.* "But she's a princess, controlled by laws of a country we never even heard of until King Alfredo's people asked us to bid on building the Miami mansion. They have rules and traditions that bind her. Everything royal would come first."

"And you don't want to be second?"

"It's more than that. That monarchy ripped my wife away from me without as much as an apology. Her dad crooked his finger and Lucy ran. I *never* heard from her again. Not because she didn't try to contact me and not because I didn't try to contact her. But because *her father* has enough power to see his will done. This is not the kind of situation a smart man gets himself into."

Ty toyed with his silverware. "So, you don't even like her anymore?"

"I *do* like her," Seth said, remembering how he'd felt talking to her on the phone in Iowa, remembering how wonderful it had felt when she'd needed him, remembering the kiss. "But I'm not going to let myself fall in love with her because she's not the person I should be married to." He paused, drinking in a long breath. "The bottom line is, no matter how sweet Lucy is, or how levelheaded she talks or how wonderful it is to be with her, I have a responsibility to Owen. He's about to be sucked into the same system that controls his mother and if I don't hang on to at least a piece of him, he won't simply lose his childhood, he'll also be lost to us forever."

"Not if you're a hands-on dad who lives with him."

"You're assuming we would stay in Porter, but we

wouldn't. If I remarried Lucy, I wouldn't be Seth Bryant anymore. I would become part of that monarchy. Which means that every time I fought for Owen's rights, I would be the rebel prince. Somebody who'd show up in the tabloids more than the *Wall Street Journal* simply because nothing would keep me from protecting Owen from being swallowed up by duty and responsibility. It would hurt Bryant Development. It would hurt Xavier Island. But most of all, it would embarrass and hurt Lucy."

Seth rose from the booth. "Her dad might not mind dragging her through the mud. But I won't hurt her. The best thing for everybody would be for us to go back to Pete's original suggestions. I need to make Lucy see that the only way her son has a shot at a normal childhood is to live with me."

With that, Seth left the diner. He debated walking the mile back to the Bryant Building, which was on the outskirts of town, but decided instead to walk the four blocks to his house and take the afternoon off. He removed his jacket and let the warmth of the late October sun warm the iciness he felt gripping his heart and soul. It went against everything inside him to fight Lucy, but that might be exactly what he could be forced to do because he would not let anyone imprison Owen.

He entered his front foyer, jacket in hand, and was surprised when Lucy bolted from the kitchen to the hall beside the stairway.

"Oh, it's you."

She looked adorable in jeans and a T-shirt with her hair pulled into a ponytail, like the one Audrey frequently wore, as if she were adapting to her new community. But Seth knew that was just an illusion. She could pretend to be a part of his world all she wanted, but at her father's command, she would leave.

Though Seth had come home for a break, seeing how cute Lucy looked after clearly outlining for his brother why he had to stay away from her, he knew he couldn't stay here. He suddenly realized that the very thing he needed to do the most for Owen—spend time with Lucy, show her he was a good guy, make her see that giving him custody of Owen assured Owen of at least a span of time of a normal life— was also the very worst thing for him to do. Spending time with Lucy only caused him to remember how much he liked her. The more he liked her, the more chance there was that he might fall in love with her for real. Then it would be hell again when she left. He absolutely refused to go through another four months of missing her so much he couldn't sleep, didn't eat and didn't care about work.

So he couldn't like her. And he also couldn't spend time with her until he regained some perspective.

"I…um…came back to see if the friend you have here helping with Owen could drive me back to the office."

Her brow wrinkled. "I thought you drove to work this morning."

"I did, but Ty drove us to the diner, and we had a sort of disagreement and I left. So now I need a ride back."

She turned toward the kitchen. "There's no one helping me right now, but I can drive you."

"You can?" he asked, following her.

"Sure." She pirouetted to face him, and the smile she gave him could have lit the darkest night. "Madelyn drove me to my six-week checkup yesterday and I'm doing great. Besides, your building isn't far, right? So it's not like I'll get lost."

Seth shook his head. "No. That's okay. I'll just walk."

"Seth!" she said, giving him an exasperated look. "What's the matter with you?"

Seth sighed. He didn't really want to be alone with her but he knew it would do him no good to argue. Plus, the office was a mile away. They would only be alone a few minutes before she dropped him off at his office and he could be away from her again.

"And what are you going to do with Owen while we're gone?"

"He's going with us. After Mildred taught me how to work the car seat, we left it installed. So it's all set up in the Chevy."

"Okay," Seth agreed.

Upstairs, Lucy slipped into the bathroom while Seth rolled Owen into a warmer sleeper and then slid him into a baby sack. When Lucy emerged with her hair out of the ponytail and combed stylishly around her face, and wearing clean jeans and an expensive-looking sweater, he laughed.

Carrying Owen, he led her out of the bedroom and into the hall. "Lucy, this is Porter. You're not going to see anyone important."

"I happen to think everybody who lives here is important," she said, as she jogged down the steps behind him. "Besides, no woman ever wants to go anywhere looking like yesterday's laundry."

Seth rolled his eyes heavenward. "I suppose not."

They walked to her car in silence. Seth buckled Owen into his heavily padded green plaid car seat, as Lucy slid onto the passenger's side of the front seat. When Seth sat behind the steering wheel, Lucy handed him the keys and turned to face Owen in the back seat.

"Ready, Owen?" Lucy asked.

Owen said nothing, but Seth laughed. "You act as if he's never done this before, but if I remember correctly he's been to the pediatrician and was also out with you yesterday to your doctor's appointment. So this is at least his third car ride."

"Yeah, but he wasn't really aware of his surroundings the first two times. Today, he'll pay attention."

Seth laughed, making the two left turns that took him to Main Street. From there, it was a straight shot to Bryant Development. "Right."

Lucy playfully slapped his arm. "He's never going to do anything if you don't encourage him and think positive!"

"And I say he should be allowed to do things at his own pace." Which, Seth suddenly saw, was actually their major disagreement. She would put Owen on the fast track to being king, while Seth wanted their son to have a life. Or, at the very least, a childhood. Still, this wasn't the time to argue. The way the plan was forming in Seth's head, he would cook duck on Saturday and make a dessert that would have her falling at his feet. Then as she ate her delicious meal, he would drop hints that if she left her son with him in Porter, the town that had already proved it would embrace Owen with open arms, he could easily raise Owen at least through his childhood. And *she* could visit him. At his house or anywhere she chose to take Owen. Her visits wouldn't be restricted the way Seth's would be. But that was what he would do on Saturday. He didn't want to get into that discussion now.

"Are you sure you're okay to drive?" he asked as he turned her car into the Bryant Development lot.

"I'm fine." She paused and smiled sheepishly. "Actually,

I'm great. Like I said. The doctor pronounced me back to normal yesterday."

Seth pulled her car to a stop at the main entrance and flipped off his seat belt. Before he could exit the vehicle, however, she touched his arm.

"Really, Seth. It's so great that you trust me. Being with you, I have the kind of life that I never, ever dreamed I could have."

"Lucy, don't…"

She smiled prettily. "Don't what? Don't tell you that I appreciate being allowed to stand on my own two feet? Most men would love hearing that."

"I'm not most men."

"Yeah, I know. You cook. You run a company. And you're the most sexy guy on the face of the earth. And you still let me be me." She bent across the seat and gave him a quick, smacking kiss on the lips. "Thanks."

Seth knew she only intended to give him the quick kiss, but sitting this close, their chemistry hummed between them, along with too many unspoken longings. Unable to control himself, he slid his hand behind her neck and pulled her forward again so he could bring her mouth to his and give her the kind of kiss he'd yearned to give her the night before.

He pressed his lips to hers, then urged her mouth open with a nudge from his tongue. She didn't protest or hesitate. She opened her mouth, slid her arms around his neck and snuggled against him as she had when they had been married.

Liquid fire danced through Seth's blood. Flames of desire licked at his nerve endings. He deepened the kiss, she nestled herself more tightly against him and every coherent thought Seth had vanished. Lucy was beautiful and smart and the mother of his child; right at this minute, he wanted nothing more in his life than to make love to her.

But when he slid his palm along the underside of her breast, her sigh brought him back to reality. He couldn't make love to her. Letting his hormones rule was how they had gotten into this mess in the first place and he couldn't afford to have the mess get any worse. Too much was at stake. He might risk the pain of another inevitable breakup, but he couldn't risk Owen's future.

He pulled away. "Drive slowly and carefully and call me when you get home so I can stop worrying."

Looking up at him with round brown eyes that glistened with desire, Lucy said, "I'm a big girl, Seth. I can take care of myself."

Seth nodded, then pushed open the car door. He didn't disagree that Lucy could take care of herself. The problem was that her father—or her country—wouldn't let her.

Traveling home the day before, he had called Pete Hauser. After six weeks of digging into Xavier's laws, Pete firmly believed that if they couldn't get jurisdiction in Arkansas, Seth wouldn't be fighting Lucy for custody; he would be fighting an entire darned country.

Chapter Seven

Lucy wasn't in the mood for company when Madelyn and her mother arrived at Seth's kitchen door after she had returned from dropping off Seth. Madelyn wore a navy-blue suit, indicating she was probably taking her lunch break from work, and had brought Sabrina in her baby carrier. Penney wore the official "outfit" of most Porter residents—jeans and a sweatshirt.

"Hi!" Lucy greeted, striving to be cheerful, but she couldn't seem to focus on anything but the fact that the kiss Seth gave her in the car was more like the kisses they'd shared in Miami. Yet, it had been different, too. In Miami, Seth had kissed her until neither one of them could think. Today, he'd stopped. He'd also gotten angry with himself for kissing her. It was obvious from the way he'd slammed the car door.

She had been absolutely thrilled that he'd kissed her. She thought the spontaneity of it proved they had deep feelings for each other and she'd let herself go and enjoyed every blissful second of being close to Seth again. She'd returned his kisses like a woman greedy for affection and would have melted if he'd told her he loved her. Heck, she would have melted if he told her he *liked* her.

Instead, he'd gotten angry with himself.

"Hey," Madelyn said, bringing Lucy back to the present. "We heard you and Seth formed some kind of truce last night."

Lucy hadn't expected that to stay a secret long. Not because the ladies were gossips, but because they considered themselves part of her team and teams kept members informed. She also didn't mind talking about this part of her relationship with Seth. These women were her friends. They were the people who were helping to assure Lucy she could care for Owen. She just hoped the discussion didn't trip over into things she didn't understand. Like a man who got angry with himself for kissing her.

"We didn't really call a truce. We formed a team," she said, closing the kitchen door behind her guests. "There's fresh coffee."

Madelyn set Sabrina's baby carrier on one of the chairs by the table and then pulled Sabrina out of it and into her arms.

Penney walked to the coffeepot. "We want details."

Lucy shrugged. "Seth came home unexpectedly late last night. Owen was screaming. I hadn't called anyone for help because I was trying to calm him myself." She smiled wryly. "I need to be able to care for him totally alone, or my father will declare me only partially suitable and I'll find myself fighting a nanny for time with my own son."

Madelyn glanced at Lucy. "Doesn't that bother you?"

"Of course! That's why I'm working to be able to care for Owen alone. I don't want a nanny."

Madelyn shook her head. "No. Not the nanny thing. I'm talking about the fact that your dad isn't just your dad. He's your supreme commander or something."

Glad the subject had drifted away from Seth, Lucy said, "It used to bother me, but now I know I can't change it so I've accepted it."

"It just seems so odd," Madelyn said.s "You're living like a normal person here, but I know you soon have to go back to a castle and be your dad's obedient subject, willing to raise Xavier's future king under the present king's dictates."

Lucy knew exactly what Madelyn was saying. Raising Owen required that she give up her own life and now that Seth had kissed her twice, that loss wasn't as simple as it had been only the day before.

She knew that the opportunity to lead a normal life had been part of what had attracted her to Seth. She hadn't precisely forgotten that her child would be heir to the throne. It was more that babies had seemed so far down the road that she'd honestly believed she would have a few years of being only Mrs. Seth Bryant before she would add mother of the future king to her roles.

But with her and Seth, everything seemed to be on a fast track. Getting pregnant the first time they made love confirmed that. Long before she had a chance to really sample what a normal life could be like, she was committed to the monarchy again.

Still, she didn't mention that to Madelyn. The last thing she wanted was for her friends to worry that she would be unhappy when she and Owen returned to Xavier Island.

So she smiled and waved a hand. "Miss Madelyn, are you forgetting that I'm royalty? There are servants who do my bidding. My country pays for my wardrobe. It's not exactly a hardship to be a princess."

Madelyn and Penney laughed and Lucy skillfully shifted the discussion to new things she needed to learn about caring for Owen. But during the next hour, she watched her two friends. Not only were they smart and kind, living exactly the lives they wanted to live, but they also really were her friends. And they weren't the only ones. Audrey was like her best friend, and Mildred, well, Mildred was becoming a surrogate mother.

If she were free, Lucy knew she could have settled in this small town with Seth and been very, very happy. But she wasn't free. She was a princess. She couldn't live here forever, and she couldn't imagine that Seth would want to leave.

More than that, though, she didn't know how Seth would handle living as a royal. Even if he could handle the pageantry and even the media, eventually he would realize that as her husband he would be required to be an obedient subject. She couldn't see Seth bowing to anyone.

When the clock struck two, Madelyn rose. "Well, my lunch is over. I've got to get back to work." She faced Penney. "Can you take Sabrina to her nanny?"

"I could, but I'd like to keep her with me for a while longer," Penney said, taking the baby from Madelyn.

"That's fine," Madelyn said as she slipped into her suit jacket. She kissed Sabrina's cheek. "Mommy will see you at about five-thirty." Sabrina cooed and Madelyn left.

Envious of Madelyn's freedom and the confidence she had in Ty's love, Lucy stared after her as she left the kitchen, closing the door behind her.

"She really does have the best of both worlds," Penney commented, obviously reading Lucy's thoughts from the expression on her face.

Lucy smiled. "Yes, she does."

"And so could you," Penney said, catching Lucy's hand to get her attention. "The thing that strikes me with you and Seth is that you're both looking at your situation as if it's all or nothing. Has either of you ever thought about making a compromise?"

Lucy shrugged. "The way I see it, there isn't a compromise. I'm the mother of a future king. I must raise him according to the dictates of our monarchy. And I don't know if Seth's ever considered a compromise because we've only really talked once since I've been here and that was last night."

Penney frowned. "You don't think that's odd?"

"No. He hasn't been home much in the past five weeks."

"But even when he was home, you didn't talk?"

Lucy shook her head.

"Why not? Really, Lucy, why haven't you talked with Seth?"

Lucy took a quiet breath. "I didn't want to hurt him. Because we were being honest last night, I had to tell him that he'll only see Owen if he flies to Xavier Island…"

Penney gaped at her. "Are you kidding?"

"No. I'm not sure of Owen's duties, but I expect my father will insist he live on Xavier. But that's only half the story. I explained the situation to Seth last night, but this morning he acted as if he hadn't heard. But I'm beginning to see that's his way of dealing with things. He pretends everything's okay when he's the most hurt." She smiled sadly. "Seth is a nice guy. Actually, he's a great guy. He doesn't deserve what's about to happen. In fact, he didn't deserve anything that happened to him after he got involved with me."

"Then fix it!"

"I can't."

"I don't believe that," Penney said, settling Sabrina when she began to fuss.

Lucy fiddled with her coffee spoon. "It's true. And I think Seth recognizes it's true. He's pretending that nothing's wrong because he knows there's no way we can make this okay and no point in arguing."

"No point!" Penney said, suddenly irate. "You have a son!"

"Exactly. If this were just about me and Seth, I could probably push and push and push until Seth admitted he wanted me again. But I'm part of something bigger than myself. I don't have the luxury of freedoms that you and Madelyn take for granted. I wasn't even at liberty to get married because I was betrothed."

"But you're not betrothed now, right?"

"No. Our pregnancy nullified the betrothal agreement."

Glancing at Owen, Penney tilted her head, thought for a few seconds, then said, "You know, Lucy, I'm not a lawyer or anything but don't you notice something funny here?"

"About what?"

"Well, from Owen's date of birth, it's pretty clear you were pregnant before you were married, and you said your pregnancy nullified your betrothal, so doesn't that mean your pregnancy nullified your betrothal *before* you got married?"

Confused, Lucy said, "I don't know. I guess…"

Penney rose from her seat, taking fussy Sabrina with

her. "If I were you, I think I'd call a lawyer. Somebody who knows your country's laws. Better yet, somebody who knows your monarchy. Because the way it looks to me, you and Seth are still married."

When Seth arrived home that evening, Lucy met him at the door. Wearing the form-fitting jeans and a simple red top she'd worn when he'd come home that afternoon after his argument at the diner with Ty, and with her thick dark hair hanging loose and free, she looked like every man's fantasy come to life. And every instinct Seth possessed bounced to attention. After the way he'd kissed her before he'd gotten out of the car that afternoon, he fully expected her to kiss him hello.

Instead, she took a quick breath and asked, "Are you starving?"

He wasn't sure what he would have done if she had kissed him. After all, he knew he'd confused her. He'd been in the process of explaining to her that there couldn't be anything between them when she'd kissed him to thank him, and like a man totally unable to control his hormones, he'd kissed her.

His self-preservation instincts had propelled him out of the car before he kissed her again...and probably again, and then God only knew what would have happened. But the bottom line was when the opportunity to kiss her had presented itself, he hadn't been able to resist it.

That meant he had to cover all his bases to ensure he didn't make another wrong move. He peered at her. "I won't faint away and die if we don't eat this second, but I am hungry."

"I have a casserole in the oven that can wait and I'd like a few minutes to talk with you."

She wanted to *talk*. Great. The perfect opportunity to really stick his foot in his mouth.

Or he could use this as a chance to stand firm in his decision not to get involved again.

Better plan. Much better plan.

He shrugged out of his suit coat and hung it on the newel of the foyer stairway. "Where's Owen?"

"Sleeping. And the baby monitor's on."

"Okay. Let's go to the den." Realistically…what could happen in a den? Sure, it had a couch and a chair, but it also had walls lined with books. Boring books about building and development. *Nothing* would happen in his den.

After walking down the slim corridor, they stepped into the large, comfortable room and Seth motioned for her to sit on the brown leather sofa. It didn't escape his notice that she sat in the middle, making it impossible for him to sit anywhere but on the chair—unless he wanted to sit right beside her.

He glanced at her pretty red shirt, her glorious bounty of hair, her plump lips.

Yeah, as if he were going to be that stupid. He sat on the chair, feeling incredibly foolish for not being able to control a couple of base instincts that were typically controlled very well by most men.

"What do you want to talk about?"

"Almost immediately after I left Miami in January, I began having bouts of morning sickness."

"Are you telling me that you knew almost immediately that you were pregnant?"

"No. At the time I thought I had the flu. I called you one night for a little sympathy, but my assistant told me that you weren't available."

Seth nodded. "And we both know why she lied."

"Yes, my father told her to do whatever she had to do to keep us apart."

"Because he didn't want us to be married."

Lucy tilted her head in agreement. "For the most part. But he also didn't want you hanging around Xavier Island too long or you would have realized something fairly obvious."

Seth's eyes narrowed. "And what's that?"

Lucy drew a quick breath. "Our pregnancy predates our marriage."

Seth almost sighed with relief. *This* he could handle. "Nobody blinks an eye at that anymore."

"Well, my dad blinked because our pregnancy predating our marriage means that technically my betrothal was nullified before we got married, so the betrothal couldn't prevent our marriage."

Seth sat up in his seat. "Are you telling me we're still married?"

Lucy drew another breath and Seth braced himself. Every time she needed air in this conversation, it was because she was about to tell him something horrible.

"Yes. I called a barrister this afternoon and after I told him Owen's birthday and explained that I was clearly pregnant before we got married, he told me that according to the laws of Xavier Island, my betrothal could not be grounds for an annulment because technically the minute I got pregnant, the betrothal was cancelled. And without grounds, there is no annulment. So, yes. We're still married."

Seth felt his mouth fall open. He couldn't have spoken if his life depended on it. They were still married! *Married.* Now he wasn't just trying to keep his hands off the woman to whom he was unreasonably attracted. He had to keep his hands off his *wife!*

He put his elbows on his knees and rested his head in his hands. "Dear God." Around Lucy, the air was sweeter, the sky bluer, and every day with her he experienced a joy the likes of which he had never known. Now, she was telling him he could have it all back. He could have the laughter, the joy…the sex.

And the only price he paid was that he become a member of her family.

No. Not her *family.* A *monarchy.* And their child was to be Xavier's next king.

Owen was already smack dab in the center of trouble. And he had no advocate. No one to fight for his rights, except Seth.

This time, Seth was the one who drew the life-sustaining breath.

If Lucy hadn't responded so eagerly to his kiss that afternoon, Seth wouldn't be worried. But she had responded. The spark of attraction was alive and well for both of them. And they were still married.

He bounced out of his seat and began to pace. "So what do we do now?"

Lucy watched him for a second, then said, "Well, I don't think we should make any rash decisions."

Seth spun to face her. "That's a good idea."

"After all, we have been apart for eight months."

"Right!"

"And I have a feeling that if we don't petition the courts to nullify the decree for the annulment filed in Xavier because of the betrothal, my father certainly won't do it."

"So our marriage continues to be annulled?"

"No, eventually we would have to address this." She met his gaze. "We can't live a lie, Seth."

Silence fell as disappointment trembled through Lucy. She reminded herself that she had had hours that afternoon to get accustomed to the fact that they were still married and that was why she had reached the acceptance phase before Seth. But that didn't dull the pain of realizing from his behavior that he didn't want to be married to her anymore.

It wasn't because he didn't *want* her. She knew from his kiss that afternoon that he wanted her. Which meant her original assessment had been correct. He didn't want to be married to a princess. In the eight months they had been apart, he had had enough time to realize the full ramifications of her being a member of a monarchy and he wanted no part of it.

He wouldn't fight for her. He wouldn't cross her dad for her. He wouldn't take a title, move to Xavier or change one iota of his life for her.

Which, now that she really thought about it, very clearly said he didn't love *her.* He might love her body, or maybe being with her, or even the way he felt when he was with her, but he didn't love *her.*

Well, fine. She was who she was. She could not change who she was. And, when the time came, she would give him the divorce he wanted. For now, she simply intended to get out of the room with her dignity.

Pasting on a smile, she rose from the sofa. "I'm going to check on the casserole."

"Good. Great," Seth said, feigning a gaiety she knew he was far, far from feeling. It was killing him that he was still married to her, and that was killing her.

Because the other thing she had had time enough to figure out that afternoon after she had spoken with the barrister was that she still loved Seth.

Chapter Eight

They ate supper in complete silence, though Seth wasn't sure why Lucy was upset. He hadn't really said anything negative. He'd remained somewhat neutral in his reaction. So he knew he hadn't said or done anything to upset her.

It took him until after eight, when they were bathing Owen for bed, that Seth realized that Lucy wasn't *upset* but *unhappy.* The only reason he could think of that she would be unhappy would be that she had expected him to respond differently to her announcement that they were still married.

Which puzzled him. Never in a million years would he even have considered that she wanted to be married to him. Sleep with him, yes. Live with him, maybe. But not be married. After all, when the chips were down, when Lucy's father instigated the scheme to prevent them from getting back together, neither one gave the other the benefit of the doubt. Both instantly assumed the other had gladly given up on their relationship. People who loved each other didn't jump to those kinds of conclusions. So, they didn't love each other. They shouldn't have married. And both should have common sense enough not to repeat the mistake. Even if he didn't have to protect Owen, he would have serious second thoughts about staying married. She should, too!

After sliding Owen into a sleeper, Seth kissed his son's forehead and left the room so Lucy could feed him a bottle before putting the baby to bed. He went to his den and tried to focus on work, but he couldn't. It was ridiculous for Lucy to want to be married again.

Frustrated, he tossed his pencil to his desk and went to look for her. He found her in the kitchen, cleaning up the supper dishes.

"It's a little late to be doing dishes."

She didn't turn around, but kept stacking dirty plates into the sink, which was rapidly filling with soapy water. "Then why didn't you do them before this?"

He smiled to himself. She had a point. "I'll help."

"Don't bother."

He grabbed a dish towel anyway, deciding it was good that they had something to do while they talked. They had to venture into the subject of their marriage. He had to tell her he believed it was ridiculous for them to even consider staying together.

"Okay, look," he said, when the first dish slid into the drainer a little too roughly. "I think I know why you're mad."

"I'm not mad."

"Okay. Maybe you're not mad, but you are unhappy and you're not treating me normally. I think it's because I didn't react the way you thought I should when you told me we were still married." He put the dish he'd just dried into the cupboard to his right. "But the truth is. I didn't really react. I wasn't positive or negative. I was neutral."

"Of course you were. That's your answer to everything. Wait and see."

"Whoa, whoa, whoa," he said, then wondered why he was doing this. She was angry. Talking was making her more angry. It seemed insane to go any further. Still, he couldn't stop himself. "What the hell kind of comment is that?"

"It's the truth."

"It's not the truth! I face things head-on."

"Oh, yeah?" she said, pulling her hands from the dishpan with such force she splashed soapy water on him. A small mountain of bubbles peaked on his chest. "Then why have you been away for the past five weeks?"

He glanced away from the suds to glare at her. "For business!"

"Are you sure it's not because you were afraid of how our visitation discussion would turn out, so you simply avoided it?"

"Yes. I'm sure."

"I think that's a lie. The whole time you were gone, I sensed something of a conspiracy behind why you were staying away…"

"Okay, Princess, you want the truth? Here's the truth. There was a conspiracy behind why I was staying away. But it wasn't fear of discussing visitation. It was fear of making you mad."

"Making me mad?" This time she shoved her hands into the water with too much force, but the result was similar to when she had pulled her hands from the dishpan too quickly. Seth got splashed with soapy water.

He didn't think she was doing it on purpose, but none-theless he was careful when he said, "Yes, I was afraid of making you mad and having you leave before we really had a chance to work anything out."

She gaped at him, but in the way that combined royal arrogance with female disbelief. If the conversation wasn't so serious, he might have laughed.

"Do you think I'm that spoiled, or is it that you think I'm prone to temper tantrums?"

If she had hit him with soapy water again, he would have thought her prone to temper tantrums. Since she didn't, he decided to officially declare the first two splash episodes accidents.

"How the hell am I supposed to know what to think about you? I knew you two weeks before we got married. We were married for two weeks. Then your dad summoned you and, Poof! you were gone."

When she caught a handful of suds and tossed it at him, he took back his earlier assessment. She was mad and she really was grabbing the only available weapon. He was glad they weren't stacking wood.

"And you never came after me! You were free to travel. *I* was not. Yet you never bothered to try to see me."

He ducked the next handful of bubbles. "Yes, I did! But I couldn't get into the palace. Hell, I couldn't even get onto the road that led to the palace. They were waiting for me at the airport. I was taken into a small room where I sat for two hours until a representative from the monarchy ar-rived and told me that I wasn't welcome. They virtually es-corted me onto the next flight to New York."

She finally faced him. "Really?"

The relief in her eyes was so intense that Seth's breath

caught. His not coming after her—or her not being told that he had tried to come after her—clearly had hurt her greatly. He thought she had wanted out of the marriage, so he envisioned her dancing at balls and playing tennis with dukes and earls. Seeing that she had been hurt squeezed his soul and he couldn't let her go on believing he had inflicted that kind of pain on her.

"Yes. I came after you. What we had was…" *Great. Wonderful. Perfect.* But he couldn't tell her that because then he would have to explain why he didn't want it anymore. He would have to tell her that he hated the world she lived in and intended to protect Owen from getting sucked into it. Or, maybe more to the point, he felt compelled to protect Owen from being *exploited* by her monarchy. If he was getting soaked for the little disagreement over why he had been gone for five weeks, he was fairly certain she would drown him if he told her he viewed her family as the enemy.

Still, he didn't need to tell her that. He only had to be careful about how he described their time together. He caught her gaze and quietly said, "What we had was very special."

This time, the handful of water she threw bounced across his cheek. "Special!" She gaped at him "You expect me to be happy that you think we were special? You told me you loved me! You told me you had never felt about anyone the way you felt about me…" She paused, her eyes narrowed; then some kind of realization dawned and she gasped. "You stereotypical American playboy! You *used* me!"

"I didn't use you!" He hadn't. He had meant every word he had said to her. Hell, he was so smitten with her he could have written sonnets. "But it won't do any of us any good to rehash our relationship."

"Why not?"

"Because."

Waiting, she crossed her arms on her chest and Seth's attention tumbled to her breasts. Vivid images and memories came back to him. And he knew that all he had to do was say the right words now and they could be sleeping together tonight.

But then he really would be using her because he knew he couldn't stay married to her.

He drew a noisy breath. "Come on, Lucy, we can't be married. We really can't. I don't fit into your world. And you…" He almost said, "don't fit into mine," but the truth was she fit perfectly. Standing by his sink, wearing jeans and a red top that was sexy without even trying, she could have been any American wife, doing the dishes with her husband. Unfortunately, she wasn't allowed to fit in his world. And any day now her father could arrive and take her away.

"And you can't stay in mine."

He expected her to realize the truth of that and her eyes to fill with tears at the hopelessness of their situation. Instead, her spine straightened and her eyes darkened with anger. "So you're making all the decisions?"

From the day he'd met her, she'd stood up to him and gotten her own way more than he had gotten his. Her being assertive now brought back some memories of other times she'd taken control and, unfortunately, those also involved bubbles, except those were in a bathtub with the two of them in it.

He forced the memories out of his head. "I *have to* make the decisions I think are right for me."

Grabbing a dish towel and drying her hands, Lucy took

the two steps that separated them. She was so close he could feel the heat of her anger.

"Without consulting me?"

Response to her nearness rattled through him. He never could be within a hundred feet of this woman without thinking about a dark room and silk sheets. She was playing with fire by pushing him right now.

"At this point, it's not wise for me to consult with you."

"Why?"

"Because if I consult with you, we're going to get too close and if we get too close we're going to…" He didn't bother finishing his sentence. He bent his head and kissed her.

Her lips tasted like heaven. The body he hauled against his felt like home. And he finally understood that they were fighting not just because they were on opposite sides of the fence, but also because they were both tired of battling the attraction that raged between them.

He couldn't stop his hands when they decided to roam across her back, down the curve of her waist or to her breasts, but he felt the answering exploration of her hands on his back, his torso and his chest. Every brush of her hand was charged with meaning. Her slight sighs of pleasure rolled through the room like thunder, alerting him that things were getting out of control. Every time they kissed, something like a nuclear explosion went off in Seth and he couldn't seem to stop the resulting ripples of reaction. He kissed. He touched. He tasted. He wanted. He wanted *everything*.

But did he want all this at Owen's expense? His son was an innocent baby who would be exploited by a heartless juggernaut of a monarchy. And Seth was his only line of defense.

He pulled away. "*That's* why I have to stay away from

you." With that, he turned from their embrace and walked out the door without caring that the dishes weren't finished. Having her tell the neighborhood ladies that he'd skipped out on kitchen cleanup was the least of his worries. Saving his son, protecting his son, was the greatest. And he wasn't going to fail.

The next day, upset about her argument with Seth, Lucy couldn't stand being cooped up anymore and she put Owen in a stroller, locked Seth's house and pushed her son the short distance to Main Street. In spite of the fact that it was the last day of October, Halloween in the United States, the day was warm, almost muggy. She stopped to remove her cardigan sweater, glancing at the houses around her.

The homes on Seth's street where all new. Rambling two-story houses with decks, skylights and sunrooms, they spoke of the extra money Bryant Development had brought into the community. The homes on the next street were mostly split-level and ranch houses. They would have been built right about the time Bryant had begun to employ people, from what Audrey had told her. The next street held Cape Cods. Older houses built in a time that wasn't so prosperous.

Main Street was a mishmash of old and new buildings. The fast-food restaurant and convenience store were new. But the diner, hardware store and dollar store were decades old. It was clear from the town's layout that Bryant Development had taken great pains to assure that Porter didn't grow too quickly to lose its charm.

As she walked down Main Street knowing that Seth and Ty Bryant had been behind most of the improvements she saw, Lucy suddenly realized something that she hadn't really understood before this. Seth and Ty weren't born to wealth and privilege. They had created it. And not just for themselves, for their entire town. Seth had the sophistication to fit into her world, even if he didn't believe it. But he had responsibilities here. In Porter.

In asking Seth to become part of her world, she wasn't simply asking him to step into a society totally different from any he'd ever encountered, she was also taking him out of a community that desperately needed him.

Preoccupied with her thoughts, Lucy entered the grocery store and didn't see Mildred until she almost bumped into her.

"Well, hello, there Mr. Bryant," Mildred said, pulling Owen out of the stroller to cuddle him before she reached out and hugged Lucy. "What are my two favorite people doing at the grocery store today?"

"We're going crazy sitting at home."

Mildred laughed. "I wondered how much longer you would be able to stand being stuck in the house!"

Lucy grinned. "I never realized a baby could keep a person so busy you couldn't get out."

"And you're still feeling good?"

"I have never felt better in my life, Mildred."

"That's my girl." She turned toward the soap aisle and hooked her free arm through Lucy's. "What are we shopping for today?"

"Fresh fruit. Vegetables. Nothing fancy."

"Not thinking of making a special dinner for Seth?"

"No."

One of Mildred's cosmetically arched brows rose. "Really? From what I heard from Penney yesterday, the two of you had a little discussion about the possibility that you and Seth might still be married."

Lucy gasped, grabbed Mildred's forearm and glanced around to be sure no one was within hearing distance. "Don't say that!"

"So it's true."

"Yes and no. The annulment order is still in place, but we can have it set aside." She winced. "Actually, we have to officially have it set aside because it's not valid. The barrister I spoke to yesterday has already started the process."

Mildred gave Lucy a confused look. "You want to put that in English?"

"Once you sort through all the paper and come to the end of all the legal proceedings, we're still married. But Seth doesn't want to be, so we're going to have to get a divorce."

"All right. This is just insane," Mildred said, pulling Lucy a little closer to assure that no one overheard them. "Lucy, honey, you love Seth. He—at the very least—likes you. And you have a child. Finding out you are married should be a good thing."

Lucy smiled sadly. "I thought it was. But Seth reacted differently than what I expected. He talked about not fitting into my world, and how being involved with me didn't work, and walking to the store today I saw his point."

Mildred gaped at her. "You *are* insane. You listen here, Mrs. Bryant," she said, obviously deliberately using the name to bring home her point. "You go home and spend time with you husband and son and then seduce that man. Let everything else work itself out!"

"But…"

"I don't want to hear it."

"It's just that…"

"Lucy, do you love him?"

Backed against a grocery shelf, with the woman she

was coming to consider the closest thing to a mother she'd ever had demanding an answer, Lucy had to admit the truth. "Yes."

"Then get home and do what I told you."

"I can't just seduce him!"

Mildred sighed. "What? You want a setup? I'll give you a setup. Tonight is the night of Porter's annual Halloween Costume Party. Take him to the party, have a few drinks and voilà, nature will take care of itself."

When Lucy didn't reply, Mildred enticingly offered, "I'll babysit."

Lucy took a quick breath. "Okay, I'll do it!"

Chapter Nine

Seth worried all day about the evening alone with Lucy. His power to resist her was clearly slim to none. Yet they were living together. When he opened the door to his home that evening and didn't smell dinner cooking, he knew she was angry with him but decided that was good. He might have to go to the diner for takeout, but at least he didn't have to worry about saying—or doing—something that would complicate a relationship that was already too complicated.

"Lucy," he called, yanking on his tie to loosen it.

As if by magic, she appeared at the top of the stairs. "Hurry up, Seth. You're going to be late."

Dressed in a red creation of some sort, Lucy was a vision. The abundant skirt of the dress puffed out from the waist and flowed to below her ankles. She always looked amazing in red, but in this particular dress she could stop traffic. He stood transfixed at the bottom of the steps, then he saw the tiara on her head and his heart stopped. She looked as if she were dressed to be going to a formal royal event; all he could think was that her dad was here.

He cautiously asked, "What are you dressed for?"

"There's a costume ball at the fire hall tonight!"

Filled with relief, but still a bit confused, he stared at her.

"I'm going as a princess."

That made him laugh. "Are you kidding me?"

She smiled and started down the steps and Seth's heart began to drum. Not only was she about to be within reach of his itching hands, but also the princess comment had sunk in. She might think it funny to dress up as something she really was, but what she'd done was bring home the reality of their situation. She was a princess. He lived in a town small enough that the fire department sponsored the only event that could even remotely be considered a formal affair. For those people dressed as ghosts, various fruits and vegetables, and Fred Flintstone, it wasn't even a formal affair. She couldn't have more clearly demonstrated that she didn't belong in his world if she'd drawn a picture or written an essay.

But as she got closer, he couldn't help but notice how beautiful she was. The minimal amount of makeup she wore enhanced her delicate features, making her brown eyes darkly mysterious. His gaze involuntarily slid to the enticing curve of her breasts as they peeked out of the juncture of the two sides of the halterlike top of her dress. She stopped in front of him and he smelled her cologne.

"I know I can't talk you into a costume, so throw on jeans and a sweatshirt."

"I can watch Owen in these," he said, pointing down at

the dress shirt and trousers he had worn to work that day, but his words were slow, his mind sluggish. This close to her when she was so beautiful, so regal, he felt hypnotized.

"Mildred's watching Owen!" she said with a bubbly laugh.

She floated past him on her cloud of filmy red material and, mesmerized, he turned, his eyes following her as she walked down the hall toward the kitchen.

"Come on! Go get dressed or we'll be late."

That was enough to bring him out of his trance. "*We'll* be late?" he asked, then laughed. He'd worried about being home with her all night, then, when he saw her, his defenses had crumbled as if they were made of sand. Thank God she'd finally said something that flipped the switch that activated his brain.

"Princess, it's been fifteen years since I've gone to the costume ball at the fire hall. And you won't be seeing me there this year, either."

She sashayed back to him, pressed her hands to his chest and smiled up at him. "Please."

Her cologne floated around him. The skirt of her dress enfolded him. Her smile called to everything male in him.

But he couldn't have her. He didn't need to go over all the reasons again. So he focused on the fact that she wanted him to do something he hadn't *ever* done as an adult. If he succumbed and went to the costume party, it wouldn't be because he wanted to. It would be because she really did have some kind of power over him. And didn't that make him a wimp? At the very least, didn't that weaken his ability to negotiate with her?

Yes. It was time to take a stand. To refuse to be at the mercy of his sex drive.

"I'm not going."

She wiggled a little closer. Her voice became as soft as a feather. "Please?"

His chest tightened. An overwhelming desire to give her the world trembled through him.

He fought it. "No."

"Please?"

This time he was smart enough to step away. "No, Lucy. Do you think I'm some kind of simpleton that you can flirt with and I'll fall at your feet?"

"I don't think you're a simpleton and I don't expect you to fall at my feet," Lucy said and smiled prettily. "I think you're my friend and I need an escort. Is it so much to ask you to do that for me?"

Oh, dear God, she'd brought out the big guns. Logic and friendship. Still, it wasn't wise for them to get too close, and no matter how she sliced it, she was still coercing him to do something he didn't want to do. And he was done being coerced. Especially by her. Once again, it was time to take a stand.

"No." He started up the steps, away from her. His days of being a manipulated man, at the mercy of his libido, were over. "Call Mildred and tell her I'm watching Owen. You go and have a good time."

In the master bedroom, he grabbed Owen from his crib, checked his diaper and then hurried over to the guest room. He laid his son in the center of the bed and began to change into something more practical for caring for a baby.

"I didn't mean to hurt your mother," he said and Owen smiled up at him from the sea of yellow flowers in the print of the bedspread. "But there are some things that a man doesn't do and one of them is cave just because a woman flirts." He shrugged out of his shirt and tossed it into the yellow bathroom.

Owen cooed.

"I'm glad you understand. And while we're at it, I might as well tell you a few other things. Your mom and I seem like a good match on the surface, but we're really not. She's a princess, and though I'm not exactly a pauper," he said, glancing around at the spare bedroom that had more amenities than most people's master bedrooms, "I'm not a prince, either."

Owen said nothing, only watched Seth as he hopped around the room, getting out of his dress trousers and jumping into clean blue jeans.

"You, on the other hand, are someday going to be a king. And though you probably think that's great," he added when Owen cooed loudly. "There are drawbacks. For one, I hear your granddad, the current king, is a real son of a…" Catching himself he quickly shifted gears. "Your granddad is a real bossy guy. I don't take well to being bossed. In fact, that's part of why I'm not going tonight."

He paused again because his last statement struck him as odd. No, it struck him as *childish*. He could see fighting his libido, not going to the fire hall because he needed to overcome the attraction that pulsed between him and Lucy. But to decide not to go because he didn't want Lucy telling him what to do…well, that simply smacked of childishness.

Fully dressed in a plaid shirt and jeans, he grabbed the baby and scrambled down the steps. He didn't exactly *want* to talk to Lucy, but he did feel he should make it clear that he wasn't being childish. He was protecting them from each other.

He couldn't decide if it was a good or a bad thing when he didn't find Lucy after a quick search downstairs. Obviously she had gone to the fire hall without him—without too much of an argument, either, he realized, but then he told himself he was lucky. He really didn't want to run into her again while she was dressed in that red thing. He could only imagine what the guys from Bryant Development's leasing department would do when she walked into the fire hall wearing that dress. They might not hoot and holler, but they would stare. No, they would *ogle!* They would trip over their tongues trying to be the first to dance with her. And when they danced with her, their hands would roam…

His lungs froze. He squeezed his eyes shut. He had to stop thinking about this because he couldn't worry about anybody's reaction to Lucy ever again. She was not his wife. Well, technically she was. But it didn't matter. He shifted Owen to a more secure position on his shoulder. Owen mattered.

He set his son in the baby seat that had been permanently installed in the kitchen and began to make himself a sandwich for supper. Before he had the bread on the table, a knock sounded on the back door. Mildred entered without being invited.

"Hey, sweetie," she said, removing her coat. "You, too, Owen," she added through a cackle-filled laugh before she walked to the baby seat and unbuckled the strap securing Owen and pulled him out to hold him.

"Put him back, Mildred. I'm not going tonight."

Mildred ignored his order about Owen. With the baby cuddled into her arm, she said, "Why not?"

"Because it isn't right for me and Lucy to be playing at being a couple."

Mildred glanced down at Owen. "It didn't seem to bother you the last time around."

"That time around we were married."

"And you're still married from what I hear."

"Yeah, but we shouldn't be."

"And you're being the big, strong tough guy here, proving that you don't have to do what you don't want to do?"

"What I *shouldn't* do, Mildred. There's a big difference."

"Yeah, right," she said, walking toward the swinging door that led to the hallway. "I'm going to watch some TV with Owen until it's time for his bath."

Seth stared at the door as it closed behind her. Was there anyone who listened to him anymore?

Actually, now that he thought about it, Lucy had listened. She told him to get dressed for the party. He said he didn't want to go. And she didn't argue. True, she had given flirting her best shot, but when it didn't work, she didn't pout. She left.

He frowned. No, *he* left. She flirted with him. He rebuffed her. Then he walked up the stairs to Owen's room where he grabbed his son and went to his own room. He didn't know if Lucy had gone to the fire hall. He didn't know if she was in her room crying.

Damn! Why hadn't he thought to make sure she'd left?

With a sigh, he took his sandwich and headed for the master bedroom. Fully expecting to hear sobs when he reached the door, he was gratified when silence greeted him. He knocked twice, then called, "Lucy?"

Nothing.

He knocked again. "Lucy?"

Nothing again.

He cocked his head and opened the door a crack to

check to be sure she really wasn't in there. But the opening was too small for him to see very far into the room. So he decided to bite the bullet and go in. But when he stepped inside silence greeted him.

And so did her cologne. It shimmied through him on a wave of white-hot desire that stopped him dead in his tracks.

He had no clue what scent Princess Lucy wore, but whatever it was, it was powerful. Probably because it was expensive and made especially for her. Because she was a princess. She had more money than Seth would ever have. She had power. She was somebody and he was nobody.

He sat on the bed, wondering if that was really what bothered him about their relationship and knew it wasn't. In the real world, if Owen's future wasn't at stake, he would give Lucy a run for her money instead of running from her.

He frowned. He wasn't running from her...

Sure he was. He could not control himself around her, so he ran out of the room, out of the house...hell, he'd gone the whole way to Idaho! She was probably at the fire hall laughing to herself about that right now.

Damn! If he stayed with her, she drove him nuts. If he protected himself, it appeared as if he was running. There was just no way to win. But one thing was certain—she needed to understand that he wasn't really running from her. Or if he was, he was running from the sex thing. Not because he was afraid of her, but because he had a job to do for Owen.

He shoved the remainder of his sandwich into his mouth, left the bedroom and jogged down the stairs. "Mildred!" he yelled, rounding the stairway and heading down the hall to the family room. "I'm going out."

"Well, la-di-da," she said, emerging from the family room with Owen on her arm. "That's what I'm here for. To babysit while you go out." She batted her hand in dismissal and headed back into the room again. "Have a good time."

"I'm not having a good time! I'm going to straighten out a few things with Lucy."

"Yeah, whatever," Mildred called from the family room as Seth headed for the front door.

It didn't matter what Mildred thought, he decided, walking down his sidewalk to the driveway. But it was such a beautiful end-of-October night that, rather than take his car, he walked past it to the street. The fire hall was a few blocks away. The fresh air would do him good.

But the closer he got to the fire hall, the slower his steps became. First, though he didn't think Lucy would end up married to another Porter, Arkansas, resident, he really didn't have a right to barge in there and mess up her good time.

Still, he had been stubborn. Actually, he'd been the one who was bossy. He'd always been bossy. Ty might be the mover and shaker. He might even be the planner. But when push came to shove, Seth gave a lot of the orders.

And anybody who didn't believe that could just ask his brother Cooper.

Seth took a quick breath. Tonight was not the night to go there. He drew another breath. Tonight probably wasn't the night to go into the fire hall, either. He'd spent the past eight months down in the dumps. Incredibly lonely. And now Lucy was here, and they were still married. But he couldn't have her, so all kinds of emotions were bubbling up. He wished they would stay crammed down in the compartments he created for them, but they wouldn't!

Standing on the wide fire hall driveway, in front of the

bay doors for the fire trucks, Seth stared at the building without really seeing it. There were no right moves in his life anymore. There were no easy decisions.

In his peripheral vision, he noticed a movement and then heard Audrey say, "Hey, Seth! What are you doing standing out here?" She laughed. "You and Lucy have a fight?"

Great. "No. I just wanted some fresh air." Not a lie, since that was why he'd walked rather than driven. "Hey, Duke," Seth said, nodding his acknowledgement of Audrey's husband.

"Evening, Seth. Nice weather, huh?"

"Great weather."

"If you asked me, it's freezing," Audrey said, then tugged on Duke's arm. "We'll see you inside."

Now, this was a lie. "Okay."

Audrey and Duke walked up to the entryway of the metal prefabricated building purchased and erected by Bryant Development, opened the door and stepped inside. Seth stayed where he was, contemplating the state of confusion of his life and suddenly knowing with absolute certainty that he was at fault for at least half of it. He knew he was also to blame for Cooper leaving. He also had to accept the blame for seducing a princess. But it wasn't his fault that Owen would be a king who wouldn't have a childhood if Seth didn't fight for at least some rights. Maybe he should have thought about that eleven months ago in Miami. But he hadn't. And neither had Lucy.

"What are you doing?"

Lucy's surprised voice preceded her as she scurried down the sidewalk to Seth.

He tried to look casual, as if he took walks like this all the time. "I wanted some fresh air."

She peeked up at him, then laughed. "So you walked to the fire hall?"

"No, I just walked. It was a coincidence that I stopped at the fire hall," he began, but he paused. He'd reached his one lie quota when he told Duke he'd see him inside. For the rest of this night, he had to tell the truth. "Actually, I felt bad about what happened between us."

"Seth, there's no reason…"

He stopped her by putting his hand on her forearm. "Lucy, I'm a real stubborn, bossy guy. If you don't believe that, you can just ask my brother Cooper if we ever find him. Ty might have been the one who got into the screaming match with Cooper over Anita, Ty's unfaithful fiancée. But what nobody knows is that after Cooper stormed up to his room, I sneaked in behind him and told him to leave."

"What?"

"I told my brother to leave. The way I saw it, Ty and I did okay, except Cooper was always screwing things up."

"Why are you telling me this?"

Seth blew his breath out on a long sigh. "In the grand scheme of things when it comes to handling situations that require some tact and diplomacy, I'm worthless."

"That's ridiculous."

"No, Lucy, that's the truth. That's why I have to be super careful about how I handle this situation with us. I screwed up my brother's life. I don't want to royally mess up Owen's." He peered at her. "No pun or insult intended."

She gave him a confused look. "None taken."

"I know the end result of making a mistake. I was upset when you left me. Brokenhearted when I realized it really was the end. But nothing hurts, nothing *haunts*, like when you ruin somebody else's life like I did with my brother because I was looking out for myself."

"Seth, don't! What were you…fifteen years old?"

"I was fifteen when my parents died. I was twenty when I told Cooper to leave. I knew what I was doing. I was clearing the way for me and Ty to work without Cooper's constant arguing. Ty and I knew exactly where we wanted our company to go and Cooper never agreed. Everything with Cooper was a struggle. I look back now and realize he was only a typical rebel. But because we were running a company, everything he said and did held us back. I got rid of him so our company could explode. And it did—at Cooper's expense."

Lucy blew her breath out on a sigh. "Seth, I understand, and I even agree to an extent. You probably did do everything you did for selfish reasons. But twenty-year-olds are selfish. That's part of growing up. And Cooper could have come home anytime he wanted. While you were gone, Madelyn told me that Ty once found him and offered him his share of the company, but he refused it. This isn't your burden anymore."

"Maybe not," Seth quietly agreed. "But it was my lesson. I deserted my brother. I will not desert my son."

Obviously noting her shiver, Seth said, "You're cold. You better get back inside."

"No. I think I've had enough of Porter's nightlife. I'd like to go home to my son." She paused, then casually added, "Are you going home?"

He glanced at the fire hall door, then shook his head as if he couldn't believe he was standing there. "Yeah."

"Can I walk with you?"

He shrugged. "Sure."

They turned and began the short trek up Main Street. "You know, you're very, very hard on yourself about your brother."

"Nah, you've only heard my side of the story. I'm sure if you heard his, you'd think differently."

"I disagree. I know better than to believe you would deliberately be so cold. You might have asked your brother to leave. But it was in the heat of the moment. You're a good person, Seth." She hooked her arm with Seth's and leaned close to his warmth as they continued toward his street.

"Thanks."

"You're welcome."

They walked in silence to the turn that would take them the final distance to Seth's home. But when they were within a few feet of his driveway, Lucy said, "I'm also very glad you're my son's father." She smiled to herself because it was true. "If we train him right, Owen will make a wonderful king. He will bring about the changes my country needs. If you think about it, having you for a dad is part of that training."

"Why? Because you think Xavier needs a stubborn, bossy king?"

"Xavier already has a stubborn, bossy monarch. What we need is a king who thinks beyond the borders. Having an American father will do that for Owen."

"I guess."

They reached the stone walk and headed for the front door. "You're also the only person I trust to take on my dad."

Seth opened the front door and motioned for her to go inside. "Right. We're two bossy, stubborn people, so I guess we will be an even match in a fight."

She laughed. "You're not as stubborn or as bossy as you think. But your stubbornness isn't the point. You're a good match for my dad because you're a future-thinker, while my dad is entrenched in the past."

Seth laughed. "You are quite a sweet talker."

Walking down the stairs Mildred said, "What are you two doing home? It's not even eight o'clock yet!" Because she was empty-handed, Lucy assumed she had just put Owen to bed for the night.

"The party was lovely," Lucy said. "And I was having a good time, but I suddenly had the urge to see my son."

Mildred stared at her. "The only time you've spent away from Owen was when Madelyn held him while you were at your six-week checkup! Go back to the party!"

Lucy laughed. "No. I'm home now," she said, and suddenly had the odd sense that it was true. She was home. And she was with the man she loved, but she had no idea how she was going to keep him.

Lucy's words resonated through Seth for the next few minutes as he watched his wife haggle with an exasperated Mildred, who finally left in a huff. He and Lucy might not ever get to share their lives but they most certainly knew each other, and tonight she had been the friend to him that he needed.

He followed her up the steps and to the master bedroom where they both walked to the crib.

"Isn't he gorgeous?"

Seth sighed. "He's handsome, Lucy. Never gorgeous. I have a feeling this is one thing your dad and I will agree on."

Lucy smiled and, in the muted light of a small lamp by the bed, Seth could see the curve of her full lips, the sparkle in her eyes. No one had ever appealed to him the way she did. And as much as he'd tried to deny it when she first returned, nobody had ever been as good a friend to him, either. No wonder he had married her without a moment's hesitation. He wanted her so badly, for so many reasons, that on a subconscious level he probably knew that if he thought too long about possibilities and consequences, he wouldn't ever marry her.

But even jumping into the relationship without thought hadn't worked. All they'd ended up doing was making things worse. Her dad had hurt them. They'd spent months aching with loneliness. Now they were finally together again and it was beginning to seem foolish to deny himself the pleasure he could have with the woman he wanted so desperately.

She walked away form the crib, her gown swishing noisily. "I think I'm going to get out of this dress now."

He didn't say a word.

She laughed. "Seth, you have to leave."

"Not really."

"What? You're going to watch me strip?"

He swallowed.

"Seth?"

When he didn't answer she walked over to him. Instantly, automatically, he ran his hands from her shoulders to her wrists and caught her fingers.

She looked up at him, her eyes shining with desire and stood on her tiptoes to brush her lips against his. Need thundered through him and he swallowed but she smiled, again pushing up on her tiptoes to brush her lips across his.

He kissed her back, deeply, instinctively, letting his impulses rule. Her softness overwhelmed him as he skimmed his palms along her upper arms, but even more so when he allowed his hands to flow from her arms, around her torso to cup her bottom. His self-control plummeted to nonexistent and he marveled at that. He'd known enough women that he had to wonder how one woman could cause him to completely lose control. Because that's exactly what was happening. As her warm mouth answered the caresses of his, he felt himself spiraling further and further away from the common sense and reason that had allowed him to keep his wits about himself around her.

And closer and closer to the promise of heaven.

He deepened the kiss even more, his tongue delving into the sweet recesses of her mouth as her arms came around his waist then anchored against his back, pulling him closer as she simultaneously pressed herself against him.

He took them to the bed almost effortlessly, careful to land on the mattress himself, with Lucy on top. His fingers skimmed down the curve of her waist, kneaded her bottom and then raced up her sides again.

He didn't think she would stop him, so he wasn't surprised when she began unbuttoning his shirt at the same time that he reached for the side zipper of her gown. With every unfastened closure he felt either the electric sensation of her nimble fingers across his chest or the smoothness of her exposed flesh.

Still kissing, they touched and explored until they were topless, soft breast to hair-roughened chest. That's when he flipped them, so that she was lying with her head on the pillow and he was beside her, one leg across her legs.

He sipped at her breast and nipped his way to her tummy, but the huge skirt of her dress stopped him. She rose slightly and within seconds, her gown was gone. Without a word, she sat up and undid the catch of his jeans. Understanding her intention, he rolled off the bed, removed his pants and quickly rejoined her.

He didn't stop to think. He didn't let her think. He simply made love to her the way he had been aching to do since the first morning he'd seen her at his kitchen table. When it was over, he rolled away from her and pulled her against him. With one arm braced behind his neck, he stared at the ceiling, and long before he was ready for it to happen, real life began to tumble into his thoughts. Owen. The monarchy. The fight he was undoubtedly about to have with the very woman who had just loved him so sweetly, so perfectly.

He shifted to gaze down at her and saw the same look of recognition in her eyes that said her thoughts mirrored his own. A million things separated them. Tomorrow, they would be back to being enemies, but tonight was theirs. He bent his head and kissed her and started to make love to her again.

Chapter Ten

Seth awakened amid a tangle of sheets and pillows. He recognized the texture and knew he was in his own bed. But he didn't recognize the scent his bedclothes now bore. They smelled like heaven. He opened his eyes slowly, savoring a happy feeling, positive that it must have come from a dream because he hadn't slept in his own room for weeks. But when he realized he really was in his own bed, the events of the night before came flooding back, along with all the emotions.

Lucy.

She loved him. She hadn't said the words, but she didn't have to. She'd proved it by taking him to her bed, making love.

Though he shouldn't have been able to even close his eyes after that, he'd slept like a baby—as if this was where he belonged. Even Owen had slept through the night, content that his parents were in the same room.

Seth ran his hand down his face and stifled a sigh, keeping his movements to a minimum because Lucy was still sleeping beside him. After all the fighting he'd done with the physical lust he had for her, he'd succumbed to the most simple emotion of all. Friendship. She was the best friend he'd ever had. It took the conversation about Cooper for him to remember that, but once he had he had been defenseless. Yet that didn't change the fact that he couldn't stay married to her.

He had to get out of here.

Sliding from beneath the warm sheet, he angled himself to rise from the bed, but a movement from Lucy distracted him and he glanced over at her. Her long dark hair looked amazing on his pale sage-colored pillow. The creamy flesh of the slope of her shoulder called to him and he ran his fingers over her gently.

Touching her felt brand-new again, and he suddenly felt like Adam looking at Eve. His Eve even held an apple of sorts. But though Seth could happily give up paradise for Lucy, he couldn't sacrifice it for Owen, and that's what he would be doing. If he gave in and allowed himself the great grace of being her husband, Owen would suffer.

Lucy unexpectedly opened her eyes. She smiled at him. "Good morning."

Unable to stop himself, Seth bent down and kissed her soft lips before he whispered, "Good morning."

"Give me a second to brush my teeth and I could be persuaded to come back to bed."

Seth's heart contracted painfully. "We can't." He gave her one last lingering look, taking in every detail of her face, her sleep-tousled hair, her pink skin, then forced himself out of bed.

Lucy sat up. In the way of longtime lovers, she didn't notice when the sheet fell exposing her breasts. "Seth?"

Knowing he couldn't lie, pretend or even skirt the issue, Seth simply said, "Lucy, last night didn't change anything." He raked his fingers through his hair in frustration. "Damn it!" When one *damn it* didn't sufficiently express his anger, he said it again. "Damn it!"

She crawled across the bed and caught his hand, forcing him to face her. "Stop. I'm not asking you to commit to me. I'm only asking you to consider something Mildred's been hinting at. She's never come right out and said it, but lots of times she falls one step short of saying that maybe fate got us pregnant because we are meant to be together."

"I don't believe in fate."

She shrugged. "With everything that's happened this past year, there are days when I'm not sure what I believe in. But I do know that her suggestion does make a weird kind of sense and if we don't at least try to figure it out before we make any decisions, we may be sorry."

Seth pulled his hand away from her and combed his fingers through his hair again. "I don't see this situation as being a matter of either of us having a decision. This stopped being about you and me the minute Owen was born."

"You think it's better for Owen that his parents live apart? That we have separate lives? That we eventually marry other people?"

Though Seth had been careful not to let himself love this woman, the thought of her marrying someone else sent a surge of jealousy through him. He was so dangerously close to loving her that he knew this was the day he had to do something. Either commit or take the stand against commitment—maybe even move out of his own house while she lived here. The problem was, if he refused to commit, he might not have to move out. She could very well pack her bags and take his son. If he made her mad enough, he knew her father had the ways and means to keep him from Owen permanently. He would never see his baby again. He wouldn't see what Owen looked like as a child, a teenager or even an adult. He could pass him on the street and not know him.

Right on cue, Owen stirred. The crib moved slightly, a tiny fist appeared from beneath a rose-petal-soft blanket and a slight cry issued.

Seth turned to walk to the crib. "I'll get him."

But Lucy was already closer. Gloriously naked, totally unconcerned, she walked to the baby's bed shrugging into a silky robe. By the time she reached for Owen, the sash was tied.

"Good morning, little one," she cooed softly.

Seth's heart constricted again. If he spent another night with her, there would be no more decision to be made. He was, after all, only human. He couldn't watch her lovingly care for his baby and share nights of passion without completely falling in love. He had to get the hell out of here. He reached for the jeans he had kicked off by the bed.

"I'll go see about breakfast."

She turned and smiled. Seth's heart tumbled in his chest. "Okay," she whispered, then nestled Owen one more time before she walked to the changing table. "Warm a bottle, will you? We'll be down after I change his diaper."

The very normalcy of that froze Seth's lungs and he couldn't breathe. He could see hundreds of mornings exactly like this one. But as quickly as that picture formed, he also remembered standing in the construction trailer in Miami, hearing the knock on the door, seeing the receptionist invite the visitor in and feeling the weight of the papers on his hand as he was officially "served." Recognizing the royal seal, he had invited the man into the private office in the back, and the barrister—her father at least had had the consideration of sending a barrister, not a messenger—had explained the betrothal, the fact that Lucy wasn't able to commit and the annulment. For as happy as Lucy had made him last night and could make him this morning and maybe every morning for who knew how long, she had also been the person who had inflicted the greatest pain he'd ever known.

He reminded himself that Lucy hadn't actually instigated the behind-the-scenes events that had culminated in their annulment and reminded himself that she had instigated their lovemaking the night before because they were still married. He squeezed his eyes shut. Technically she was his, but she would never stop being a princess. And Seth would never ask her to.

He buttoned his jeans, telling himself to leave his other clothes for later. But at the door he took a breath and turned to face her.

"I don't want to talk about this anymore, Lucy. It's tearing me apart. I can't be tempted day after day and not expect to succumb like I did last night. But if this goes on, I'm going to end up falling in love with you, and if I fall in love with you, there's no one to protect Owen."

"Seth, that's not…"

"I mean it! Owen is the most important responsibility I've ever had. I will not blow this one! I cannot be involved with you. In fact, I want you to start thinking about Owen.

If you and I don't have a relationship, where do you want him raised, really? Here in Porter or on Xavier Island."

She opened her mouth to answer, but Seth stopped her. "Don't say a word right now. Just think about it. Really think about it."

With that, he left the room. Though he had told Lucy he would see to breakfast, he walked into the spare bedroom he was using, dressed and went to work. It was Saturday, but he finally understood that only keeping his distance from Lucy would save him.

That evening, Seth heard his doorbell ring. He had called his housekeeper, Belle, that morning and told her to come back to work, if only to make sure there was another person in the house to keep him and Lucy apart. He knew Belle would answer the door, but he needed a break from his work. He rose from the seat behind his desk in the den and started up the hall. Before he reached the end of the corridor, though, Belle appeared at the front door.

With her pink maid's uniform hugging her generous body and her red hair pulled into a bun, she looked the picture of an unflappable domestic. When she opened the door two men stepped inside without being invited, she jumped back with a gasp.

"Who the heck are you?" she asked, but Seth knew who they were. He'd even met them before because at one time each had been assigned to guard Lucy.

After a quick visual inspection of Seth's foyer, they stepped away from the door and a tall, dark-haired man who looked to be in his midforties entered. Wearing an overcoat atop a navy blue suit, white shirt and tie, he could have been an American businessman, but since so few businessmen had bodyguards who checked the house they were about to enter, Seth knew he was looking at Lucy's dad—King Alfredo of Xavier Island.

The big man faced Seth, smiled and shook his head. "So, you've stolen my daughter again."

Feeling more like a highwayman or a pirate than the man who had been seduced by King Alfredo's daughter the night before, Seth said, "No one steals Lucy."

"No one tells Lucy what to do, that's for sure," the king agreed, handing his overcoat to one of his bodyguards. "Can I see my daughter?"

Seth nodded. "Belle, show King Alfredo and his body-guards into the living room."

With eyes as wide as dinner plates, Belle faced Seth. "This is Princess Lucy's father?"

"Yeah, Belle, and in his country servants don't talk, so just skip on into the living room with him and get him some coffee or something."

"Brandy would be better," the king said with another smile, good-naturedly accepting that he wasn't in Xavier anymore.

Seth felt himself relax a little, but he wasn't foolish enough to relax completely, no matter how polite King Alfredo was. From the way this man had ruined Seth's life, Seth had expected to meet a guy with two horns, a tail and a pitchfork. At the very least, he thought the king would have a moustache that would give him a dark, sinister appearance. Instead, the king looked more like someone who should be posing for *GQ* or maybe modeling for Armani.

"I'll get Lucy."

Seth turned and began walking up the steps as Belle led the king and company through the dining room into the living room. Seth realized belatedly that he should have told Belle to guide the king to the living room through the corridors and not drag him through the dining room, but this was America. And protocol wasn't on his or Belle's daily agenda.

Reaching the master bedroom, he drew a quick breath, then opened the door. Lucy sat on the rocker, feeding Owen his last bottle before bed.

She smiled. Though he'd told her that morning that they couldn't have a relationship, from the expression on her face, it was clear she thought he'd come into the master bedroom because he wanted to sleep with her again. The hopeful look in her eyes nearly did him in.

"Hey."

"Hey," Seth said, then sat on the bed. "Look, I'm not sure if this is good news or bad news, but King Dad is in my living room."

He watched Lucy's hopeful look crumble.

Seth became instantly alert. "Are you afraid of him?"

She shook her head. "No."

"Hey, Luce, this is me. If I find out you're afraid of your dad and you didn't tell me, there will be hell to pay."

"No." She smiled. "I'm not afraid. I guess I was hoping the legislative session would last a while longer. Don't read into my expressions, Seth. My dad is a good man. And in spite of his faults, I love him. I'm just not quite ready for him yet."

"Well, I can probably give you another minute to get ready, then you've got to come downstairs. The king and I don't exactly have a lot to talk about."

Lucy shook her head. "Not true. You have Owen."

"Yeah. I have Owen for another…maybe…two hours

before your dad spirits him away in a private plane." At which point Seth would call Pete Hauser and tell him to file for custody and the fight would begin.

"Then, perhaps you'd like to hold him while I speak with my father alone."

Seth shook his head. "No way in hell! We're going in together."

"With Owen?"

"I can't think of a more perfect buffer."

Lucy laughed and Seth took Owen from her hands. "Are you going to change?"

She glanced at her own blue jeans and T-shirt and shook her head. "I don't think so."

Linking her arm through Seth's, Lucy walked along with him to the door, which she opened. In only a few seconds, she was standing on the threshold of the living room, looking at her dad.

"Daddy?" she said and he turned to face her.

"Lucy!" The king's long strides ate up the space of the living room and he grabbed her and hugged her.

Seth stood off to the side, holding Owen. He didn't have to wonder why King Alfredo had used all the power at his disposal to get his daughter back when she'd married Seth. He loved her. The warmth of his affection shone through his eyes as he hugged her fiercely.

But Seth also didn't have to wonder why Lucy had run home when her father beckoned. Her love was every bit as clear as she hugged her dad. The way she called him Daddy—not Your Majesty, not Father, not even Dad—said more than Lucy could ever put into words.

"And this must be Owen," King Alfredo said, stepping away from his daughter, though he didn't totally release her. Again, Seth saw the significance of the body language. He had no intention of letting Lucy go.

But Lucy also did not release her father. With one arm slid casually around his waist, she watched as the king took Owen from Seth's arms.

"Oh, my," he said, and tears filled his eyes. "Oh, Lucy."

"Isn't he wonderful, Dad?"

"He's—" the king blinked back tears "—he's perfect."

His feelings a jumble, Seth took a step back. He'd expected Lucy's dad to have horns, a tail and a pitchfork. He thought for sure he'd see a surge of anger from Lucy. Instead, he was witnessing a loving reunion.

And something became patently clear. Lucy couldn't choose Seth over everything else. Not merely because she was a princess who had duties and a life beyond anything Seth could give her, but also because she loved her dad. Choosing Seth would mean living in America. Choosing Seth would mean more than giving up a throne. It would mean living away from her dad.

He drew a quick breath. The king glanced at him. "My sources tell me you actually delivered this child."

"I called for help. No one came."

The king laughed. "No need to be defensive. I was complimenting you."

Seth relaxed, but he said, "I think I'll go check on Belle."

"No need," King Alfredo said. "At the last second, I declined the brandy."

Seth said, "Okay."

"But I do have a favor to ask."

Not knowing what else to say, Seth said, "What?"

"I would like to spend the night here so I can catch up with Lucy and visit with Owen."

"I don't have any bodyguards."

"There have been bodyguards watching your house since Lucy moved in. But to accommodate my presence, Jason," the king said, nodding at the older of the two men he'd brought inside with him, "has also arranged six men on your property."

"Oh, my neighbors are going to have a field day with this."

"Your neighbors won't know," Jason quietly assured Seth.

Not able to argue that, and not really wanting to hear details, Seth nodded. "Great."

"So, how about if we all sit down," King Alfredo suggested.

"That sounds great, Dad, but it's Owen's bedtime. Give me a few minutes to put him down for the night and I'll be back."

King Alfredo handed his grandson to his daughter. "That's fine. I think Seth and I should take a minute to get to know each other anyway."

Lucy cuddled Owen to her. "Okay," she said and walked out of the room.

King Alfredo motioned for Seth to take a seat on his own sofa and Seth's nerves began to pop. Only a man accustomed to being the leader of the pack would ask a man to sit in his own home.

"How long does it usually take for Lucy to put Owen to bed?" the king asked without preamble.

"Since he's already been bathed and fed, not long," Seth said, ungodly grateful for that.

"Then I'll get right to the point. You know, of course, that Owen must be raised in Xavier."

"Actually, I don't know anything of the sort. My lawyer feels he can be 'raised' anywhere. He also has a right to renounce his throne."

"To do what? Live in America? You Americans astound me with your arrogance. Not everyone *wants* to live here, and a king certainly wouldn't give up his throne to run a construction company."

Seth knew he shouldn't have been surprised by how much the king knew about him, but the casual reference to his private life did hit a nerve. He suspected the king had intended that.

"Make no mistake, Seth. If you fight me," King Alfredo said, "I will win. It would be a waste of time to file for custody. In fact, I had my barristers run through several scenarios of how this would probably turn out if our mutual legal actions were handled by American courts."

The king faced Jason and Jason pulled an envelope from his jacket pocket.

"After running through all the possible ways this case could go, my barristers decided that Xavier Island's claim to Owen would undoubtedly take precedence. However, we also believe a judge would give you very lenient visitation rights."

Seth stared at the man. "How many scenarios did you run?"

Jason said, "Forty-one. Including one where Lucy died and one where Lucy stayed married to you."

"*Stayed* married to me?"

The king smiled wryly. "You know that you're still married."

Seth nodded. "Yeah, I knew. I just didn't think you knew I knew."

"Even when Lucy is off Xavier Island, I know exactly what's going on in her life. An hour after Owen was born, I knew. If I hadn't believed the media would follow me if

I left Xavier Island during the legislative session I would have been here the day after Owen's birth and Lucy and Owen would be in Xavier with me right now."

Seth sat back on the couch.

"But that's beside the point," the king said. "What is on point, however, is that should you choose to stay married to my daughter, this," he said, handing the envelope to Seth, "is off the table."

Seth looked up at the king.

"It's an agreement between you and the monarchy of Xavier Island. Your son is our next king. We want him in our country. All the same, we recognize you have rights, so this agreement gives them to you."

Seth looked at the envelope and laughed. "Don't tell me you've drawn up a document that gives me every other Christmas and two other holidays to be named at a later date," he said, making fun, because he was sure the king wasn't anywhere near that generous.

The king smiled. "Actually, Seth, we're giving you the entire school year until Owen is ten."

Seth gasped. "What?"

"Our research has shown that in America, most of a child's life revolves around going to school. You probably want your son to play…" He faced Jason. "What's it called?"

"Little League," Jason supplied.

"Yes," King Alfredo said, facing Seth again. "You probably want Owen to play Little League."

Stunned to his socks, Seth swallowed. "Yes, I do."

"So, this agreement has Owen living with his mother on Xavier Island most of his first four years. You will have four two-week visits with him in that time. Then the balance shifts. He comes to live with you so you can enroll him in a preschool, and we get Owen through his summer vacation and for all royal affairs that he is required to attend. Until he's ten. When he's ten, we will negotiate again. In fact, if the deal works well, I can't see any reason why we wouldn't extend it through high school. Even college. As long as Owen's life here doesn't interfere with the things he must do for our country, you could have your son most of his life."

Astounded, Seth stared at King Alfredo. When he spoke, it was cautiously. "This is very generous."

The king smiled. "Yes, it is. But think it through. Owen living away from the palace isn't unusual. Most royal children go away to boarding school. That would even be the story the Xavier monarchy would release to the press. We could have a private school confirm that Owen is a student there if only to assure that no one looks for him. In fact, it's the perfect way to protect him. We'd sort of be hiding him here with you."

Seth stared at the papers in his hand for several minutes before he said, "The catch, though, is that I have to give up Lucy."

King Alfredo smiled as if he had expected Seth to figure that out. "Yes, you do."

"Why?"

"Because if she stays here with you, none of our stories will work. Owen will get no privacy. *You* will get no privacy. The bodyguards stationed in your yard right now will be small potatoes to what you will need."

He stared at the king, then said, "So, this is about our *privacy.*"

"And Owen's safety."

Seth nodded his agreement, but he wasn't a complete idiot, either. He hated the way the king seemed to hold all the cards. Particularly since he knew King Alfredo wasn't being totally honest. "And it's also about keeping a commoner out of your palace."

The king had the good graces not to deny it. "You wouldn't like it there, anyway."

Chapter Eleven

Seth waited until he was sure everyone was asleep, then he sneaked out of his bedroom, down the hall and directly into the arms of a bodyguard who suddenly appeared at the top of the steps.

"Excuse me, sir."

"You're excused," Seth said and tried to get around the man who had to be six foot four, probably two hundred and fifty pounds. When his beefy hand pressed against Seth's chest, Seth also knew the guy was as strong as a bull. If he pressed any harder, Seth would be on the floor.

"I think you misunderstood. I apologize for not being clearer," he said with the kind of sincerity that Seth knew wasn't faked. This guy knew how to handle the people he protected. "Now that we're locked down, no one is permitted to leave the house."

Seth gaped at him. "Are you telling me I can't leave my own home?"

"For the safety of King Alfredo…"

"Stand aside. Now," Seth said, no longer caring if anybody woke up. "This is Porter, Arkansas. Half the time I don't lock my door. You let me go or tomorrow I'll file charges."

"We've already checked in with law enforcement, Mr. Bryant. They were alerted that you accepted us in your house and on your property. You wouldn't make any charges stick."

"I'm on my way to see my lawyer," Seth said patiently.

"And you may certainly do that tomorrow morning…"

"I can't wait until tomorrow morning!"

"Then maybe you could use the phone," the bodyguard said, simultaneously apologetic and firm.

Seth stared at him and suddenly realized he wasn't going anywhere. He also knew that this was exactly why he had to sign that agreement. Right now, he was only being held prisoner in his house. In the middle of the night. When no one should want to go out, anyway. But Owen would spend his entire life like this. Answering to bodyguards who had been given orders by a king.

He took a breath. "Fine. I'll *call* my lawyer. If you'll let me downstairs."

The bodyguard stepped aside. "I'm sorry, sir."

"Right. Sorry," Seth mumbled, jogging down the steps. In his office, he dialed Pete Hauser's number and waited through four rings before his attorney picked up.

"I woke you, didn't I?"

Seth heard Pete's deep breath that told him his lawyer needed to revive himself and get his bearings. "Yeah, Seth, you woke me but, you know what? I'm getting used to this."

"I'm going to e-mail you an agreement and I want you

to find the loophole. I know there's a loophole," he said, hearing the desperation in his voice and knowing it was from his conflicted feelings about signing. Technically, the agreement only gave him the rights he and Ty had been angling for since the princess had arrived and given birth to his son on his sofa. Yet, now that he and Lucy had spent time together, taking Owen from her didn't seem right. But he also couldn't think of a compromise. Even if they split custody right down the middle, Owen would live six months of every year in a hell of sorts. Lucy herself had said that in the magazine interview Pete Hauser had given Seth to read.

On the other hand, because the king had offered exactly what Seth wanted, and so easily, Seth knew there had to be a catch.

He e-mailed a scanned copy of the agreement to Pete and waited what seemed like an eternity before Pete called him with the verdict.

"It's the strangest thing, Seth. This agreement is what I would have written for you, expecting the king to counter with his demands. Instead, he's handing you what you want."

"You don't think it's a ploy to get me to sign, and then somehow use it against me—maybe even to prove to Lucy that I betrayed her when the opportunity arose?"

"Nope," Pete said quickly, unequivocally. "The king has already signed it. And it bears the official seal of the Xavier Island monarchy. He probably signed it first to prove to you that the agreement wasn't a ploy to get your signature and then somehow use it against you."

"And it's legal?"

"It is as legal as legal gets. It's signed. And it gives you everything you want. It's as if the king doesn't want an argument from you or doesn't want to leave any reason for you to come back and bother him. Almost as if he wants you to sign and sort of go away."

"That's exactly what he wants."

"He also doesn't want you married to his daughter."

Seth smiled wryly. "No. He doesn't."

"Is that a problem?" Pete asked quietly.

"What?"

"Giving up Lucy?"

Seth took a deep breath. His house was filled with bodyguards. He wasn't in control of his own home because a king slept in one of his bedrooms. Hell, he wasn't in control of his own life! He couldn't even go up the street to see his lawyer because his house was "locked down" for the night.

If he didn't give up Lucy, this would be his life, and he knew he couldn't handle it. No. That wasn't it. The problem was that he'd never willingly walk into this trap. So there was no question that he and Lucy would never get back together.

Realizing that hurt. He saw her marrying someone else, forgetting him and having a wonderful life without him. Because that's really what would happen. A woman as beautiful and loving as Lucy wouldn't be alone for long.

When Seth didn't reply, Pete added, "I guess what I'm really asking is do you love her?"

Seth tossed a pencil across his desk. "No. I don't love her. I've been so careful not to cross that line that I sometimes think I'll explode. But, no. I haven't crossed the line."

"Good."

"Even if I had, my feelings for her almost don't matter. Right now, there are no fewer than eight bodyguards on my property. Two of them are in my kitchen making sand-wiches. I'm surprised I was allowed to shower alone. I don't know how anybody can live like this."

"Then sign. Sign this thing before King Alfredo has a chance to change his mind."

At seven-thirty, when Seth walked into the kitchen, Lucy looked up from the pancakes she was making. "My father is amazed that I can cook."

She watched Seth catch her father's gaze and panic flut-tered in her stomach until Seth said, "You've always un-derestimated your daughter." Then she relaxed. She wasn't exactly looking forward to the argument between Seth and her father, but she knew it was coming. In fact, she had been praying for it. Once they fought this out, her father would see there was no separating her and Seth and he would relent. He almost always did, when she rarely stood her ground with him. But in this case, Seth would have to be the one to stand "their" ground.

Her father said, "I haven't underestimated my daugh-ter. I believe I've protected my daughter."

"Well, this time around, I'm going to undercut you," Seth said. He walked to the stove and took Lucy's arm to direct her to the kitchen table. "We need to talk, with your dad, and I want your full attention."

His actions weren't the actions of a man about to get into an argument with her father. The panic returned and she fought it by focusing on what she was doing. "But my pancakes!"

"Will be forgotten in about two minutes."

"Seth!"

Her dad's voice was a warning growl that reinforced her

feeling of panic. This was not going anywhere near the way she had expected it would. Instead of her father and Seth being on the hot seats, she was the one in the center of things. She suddenly felt as if the kitchen floor had fallen out from under her.

"Daddy?"

But it wasn't her father that spoke. Seth did. "You can't always have everything your way, Your Majesty. I think Lucy deserves to know the truth of what we agreed to."

Lucy glanced at Seth. "You agreed to something?"

He handed her a copy of a legal document of some sort. "Your father gave me this last night. I e-mailed it to Pete Hauser. He reviewed it and told me it was on the up-and-up. The agreement is totally legitimate."

Lucy stared at him as anger heated the blood in her veins. Once again, Seth had made a decision without her. "Agreement for what?"

"Your father has virtually given me Owen to raise."

Her blood that had been heating with anger suddenly froze with fear. "What?"

"You hated your childhood," Seth said simply. "I fear for Owen. This agreement gives us a way to give Owen a normal childhood."

"How?"

"By getting a private school to list Owen on the school rolls, as if he were attending," the king said, rising from his seat at the table. "While Owen actually lives in here in Arkansas, virtually without a bodyguard."

Lucy swallowed. A trembling started in her stomach and rippled out to her limbs until every inch of her body was shaking. She caught Seth's gaze and, as always, she could read what he was thinking. His green eyes were dull with disappointment. The agreement that benefited him didn't benefit her and she knew why.

She swallowed again before she quietly said, "As long as Owen is without his mother."

"You aren't anonymous," her father reminded her. "The minute you're in the picture, Owen wouldn't have a normal life."

Lucy took a quick breath. She caught Seth's gaze again. "In other words, you traded me for Owen."

"I didn't have a choice."

The expression in Seth's eyes told Lucy that he truly believed that, which meant there was no changing his mind, and she ordered herself not to crumble. Not to cry. Instead, she straightened her shoulders. "May I read this?"

The king said, "Of course."

Seth caught her arm. "Lucy, I…"

She shook free. "I'm Princess Santos to you, Mr. Bryant. You hated that I was promised to someone as if I were a commodity. Yet you just traded me away like a sack of potatoes. You're a hypocrite," she said, then strode to the door. Head high and with every ounce of regal comportment she could muster, she walked down the hall, climbed the steps and entered the master bedroom.

When the door closed behind her, she fell to the floor and cried. The one person she'd genuinely believed understood how horrible it was to be a pawn in a global game had traded her.

Seth was inordinately glad when the king announced that he would be dining with friends in Houston that night and returning in the morning. He'd expected Lucy to come downstairs for dinner, but she didn't. He knew she hadn't eaten breakfast. He knew she hadn't eaten lunch. Now she was skipping dinner.

Recognizing that they had to talk this out and that he had to be honest and admit he'd saved Owen because he believed there was no chance for a relationship between them, not a long-term relationship, anyway, he walked down the hall to the master bedroom and knocked once. No answer.

"Lucy, come on. You have to eat."

"Go away, Seth."

"Lucy! Come on. You know I did what I had to do."

"The funny part of this is, Seth, I do know that. I understand your decision a lot better than you think I do. But because I understand I never, ever, want to see you again."

Seth stared at the door.

"Go away, Seth."

"What did you expect her to do?" Madelyn asked, totally appalled when she heard Seth's story. He'd come to Ty's house, looking for confirmation that he'd done the right thing. Instead, Madelyn had blown the whole situation out of proportion.

"What did you expect *me* to do?" Seth countered, pacing Ty's den. "Think this through, Madelyn. Owen's life would be public property if I didn't sign that agreement. The king offered me my son's life. I took it."

While Madelyn and Seth had been arguing, Ty had been reading the agreement. He finished and tossed it to his desk. "Seth is right, Madelyn. I don't think he had a choice."

Madelyn looked from Seth to Ty. "Are you kidding me?"

Ty shook his head. "The agreement gives Owen a life he wouldn't otherwise have."

"And what about Lucy?" When neither Ty nor Seth answered, Madelyn again demanded, "What about Lucy!"

Seth took a quick breath. "I've been surrounded by bodyguards for two days and they've already driven me insane. Even if I loved her—which I have taken great pains not to do—there is no future for me and Lucy. I could not live her life."

"But she could live yours," she quietly replied.

"She has duties and responsibilities. She's already proved that they come first."

Madelyn stared at him. "Are you punishing her for leaving the first time in Miami?"

"No!" Seth emphatically denied. "Madelyn, this is not about me and Lucy. It's about Owen."

"You know what, Seth? I think you're right. This isn't about you and Lucy. It's about *you*. It's about *you* refusing to compromise. It's about *you* refusing to risk."

"There is no compromise."

"How would you know? I don't think you actually looked for one. Because you're not the same guy Lucy fell in love with all those months ago. I saw you change. I saw you go from happy-go-lucky to brooding in what seemed like a weekend and I now know that's because Lucy had gone home when her father summoned her. I saw you suffer for months before you came to terms with your loss. It nearly killed you. And I think the real bottom line here isn't that you can't handle living as a royal, with bodyguards and schedules and paparazzi chasing you. The truth is, Lucy broke your heart once and you're not going to let her do it again. Even if it means hurting her more than anybody else could ever hurt her." She drew a quick, impassioned breath. "I'm glad you're not the Bryant I fell in love with." With that, she stormed out of the den.

For several seconds, silence reigned. The only sound was the tick of the grandfather clock in the foyer.

Finally, Seth said, "There isn't a compromise."

"Honestly, Seth. I wouldn't know. But I haven't looked for one because it isn't my life. And I'm not the one virtually condemning a very nice, very sweet, very generous woman to life without her child and without the man she loves." He rose from his desk. "I'm going to go settle Madelyn. You can let yourself out."

The next morning Seth tried to catch Lucy in the kitchen when she got Owen's morning bottle. Instead, he found Audrey, who told him the princess and Owen had already left for the airport.

He stared at her. "She left without giving me a chance to say goodbye to Owen?"

"Seth, from the way I hear the story, you get to raise Owen. So I wouldn't be too snotty about anything the princess does right now."

Not about to argue with Audrey when he couldn't even convince his own brother he'd done what he'd had to do, Seth turned and climbed the steps to his bedroom. Suddenly, he realized the master bedroom was his again and he changed directions.

When he entered his room, he smelled her. The shampoo. The cologne she used. He saw the empty crib. The empty closet. The room felt hollow. Lifeless.

His chest tightened. Just as it had on the horrible day in March when King Alfredo's messenger had handed him annulment papers, Seth realized with absolute certainty that he was never going to see Lucy again. Not because her father would prevent it—though Seth was fairly certain the king intended to keep Seth and Lucy as far apart as he possibly could—but because Lucy didn't want to see him.

And he didn't blame her. Though Seth knew Lucy understood that he'd signed the agreement to assure Owen had a normal life, he also knew that Madelyn was right. Seth was so darned afraid Lucy would hurt him again that he'd leaped on the first chance to save himself. Without ever once considering that he was hurting her. Or looking for a compromise.

He sat on the bed. Dear God, what had he done?

Seth jumped into his SUV and took the shortcut to the airstrip. From a distance he could see the white limo parked by the metal hangar. Off to the left, away from the grouping of private planes owned by locals, he saw the jet with the crest of Xavier Island. He pushed down on the gas pedal and he also didn't bother with roads. He drove over grass, mud and macadam and brought his vehicle alongside the limo with a spray of gravel.

With a bodyguard beside her, Lucy walked across the tarmac, holding Owen, heading for the small private jet.

"Lucy!" he yelled, jumping out of his SUV, running toward the tarmac.

She ignored him.

"Lucy!"

She continued walking to the three-stepped entry of the plane.

Seth ran toward her. "Lucy!"

Finally, she turned. "Get lost, Seth."

"Lucy, no! I made a mistake. I shouldn't have signed."

"It's too late," she said and pivoted away from him, moving toward the jet again.

He caught up to her and grabbed her arm. Her bodyguard immediately snatched Seth's hand from Lucy's arm and twisted it behind his back as he yanked Seth away from her. But Seth kept talking. "No! It isn't too late! I signed an agreement that said I would divorce you, but there's nothing in that agreement that says I can't remarry you."

Her gaze swung to his. "What?"

"I read that agreement three times last night and I swear there is no provision that says I can't remarry you."

"James," Lucy said to her bodyguard. "Give us a minute."

The bodyguard released Seth and stepped back but didn't actually leave. Lucy sighed warily. "There might be no stipulation against us remarrying, but you want Owen to lead a normal life."

"Owen needs two parents to have a normal life."

"I'm a princess. Everyone in Porter knows that. There will be no hiding me."

"Everyone in Porter knows Owen's a prince. We're not going to hide it. We're going to trust our friends and neighbors to help us."

"I have bodyguards."

"Owen will have to have bodyguards, too. I might trust my neighbors, but I'm not stupid. I simply intend to make them the cook, the gardener and the pool guy."

Lucy almost laughed. Almost. Because the truth was this was all nice, but it wasn't what she wanted. She knew Seth felt guilty about hurting her and this proposition might be his way of feeling better about himself. She also knew that any second now her dad would wonder why she wasn't in the plane and he'd either make an appearance or send someone to check on her. If Seth loved her, she had to get him to say it quickly. "Your suggestion is very clever."

He gaped at her. "Clever! It's downright brilliant! When I really thought about how *I* would protect you if you were my wife, I had lots of brilliant ideas for keeping you safe."

"And Owen."

He glanced down at the bundle in her arms. "And Owen."

She said nothing and Seth sighed. "Lucy, you are not helping things here."

"Frankly, Seth, neither are you."

"I'm giving you everything you have ever wanted. Quiet. Privacy. A normal life. Everything!"

"Not everything."

He stared at her for a few seconds, then his eyes narrowed. "What are you saying?"

"What are you saying? You come here and tell me you're going to give me a normal life. You tell me you will protect me and Owen, and that's wonderful. But it's not really enough."

He drew a breath. "Then I don't know what is."

Her suspicions were confirmed—he was only doing this out of guilt, not love. Lucy told herself she wasn't going to cry. "Then I think I had better leave."

When she turned away, she couldn't stop the tears that sprang to her eyes. Abundant and heavy, they poured over eyelids and fell to her cheeks.

She reached the steps for the jet and the pilot caught her arm to assist her up the first step. "Good morning, Princess."

Unable to speak, she nodded.

"Lucy!"

Lucy heard Seth call her name again, but this time she couldn't turn around. She let the pilot see the tears streaming down her cheeks because he was too polite and well-trained to mention them, but she refused to let Seth see her cry. All she had ever wanted was for Seth to love her. And she'd literally tried everything, but nothing had worked.

"You can't leave."

She took the second step of three.

"I can't raise Owen without you!"

She put her foot on the third step and could now see into the cabin of the jet, which looked more like a comfortable living room. Accommodations had been made for Owen, and a nurse appeared at the doorway, taking the baby from Lucy's hands.

"I love you!"

Hearing the words she'd longed to hear for too many excruciating months, Lucy froze.

"I love you," Seth said again, and this time the sincerity in his voice stopped Lucy's heart.

She spun around. He ran toward the jet.

Looking up at her from the bottom of the steps, he said, "I love you. I think I always did love you. I cannot raise Owen without you. Please, Lucy, don't leave."

Lucy raced down the steps and into his arms. "I won't," she said and kissed his cheeks as he began to rain kisses on her face. "I won't ever leave if you promise to always love me."

"I promise."

"And we'll get a cook and a gardener and a pool guy?"

He nodded. "I'll even go to your stupid island. I'll go to balls. I'll attend ceremonies." He winced. "Just tell me that you'll never force me to wear purple tights and a cape."

Lucy pulled away from him and studied his face. In spite of the seriousness of his question, she laughed. "What?"

"Purple tights. I don't want to wear anything that makes me look like something out of a comic book."

"You either have an outdated view of royalty, or you believe the pictures you saw in the fairy tales your mother read to you. Nobody wears purple tights." She laughed again. "In fact, if we force my dad to stick to his agreement, we really only have to go to Xavier a few times a year."

Seth took a breath. "Unless you want to go. You know, to visit your dad."

"You would let me?"

"Lucy, in the same way I didn't want to be a prisoner to your monarchy, I won't make you a prisoner here."

She smiled.

He smiled. Then a look of relief came to his face. "I think we did it. I think we found the compromise."

Holding on to Seth, Lucy said, "I'm glad. Because I don't think I ever stopped loving you."

"Good, because I don't think I ever stopped loving you, either. Let's grab Owen and get the heck out of here. We've got some bodyguards to hire."

"Sounds like a plan," Lucy agreed, scurrying up the steps to take Owen from his nurse. At the bottom, she caught the pilot's arm. "Take a message for my dad. Tell him I've changed my mind. I'm not going to Xavier with him. My husband and I will be at our home with our baby. He's welcome to visit anytime."

She glanced at Seth. "Right?"

"Sure, absolutely. After all," Seth said, sliding his arm around Lucy's shoulders. "He's family and in Arkansas, we take our family seriously."

Epilogue

"See, I told you you wouldn't have to wear purple tights."

"Thank God!" Seth stepped away from the mirror in the bedroom of Lucy's suite in the palace. "How do I look?"

In a tuxedo, Lucy's husband looked better than Brad Pitt and Justin Timberlake without shirts. He looked so good Lucy almost couldn't believe he was hers. But he was. When her father realized she and Seth were not parting and they intended to fight him to assure Owen had at least something of a normal life, the king had relented. He tore up the agreement Seth had signed, ordered the courts to void the annulment and decided to simply enjoy his daughter's new life.

"You'll do."

"Huh! I'll do!" Seth caught her around the waist and hauled her to him. He bent her backward, over his arm, leaned down and nipped her neck.

"Stop!" Lucy squealed, laughing and wiggling to get out

of his hold, though her tight red gown made movement nearly impossible. She wasn't even sure she'd be able to dance in this thing and couldn't believe she'd let Madelyn talk her into wearing a dress so scandalous. Especially to the reception celebrating her wedding. Of course, as Madelyn had pointed out, it would be ridiculous to wear white, so why not go all the way and wear the color that most typified her relationship with Seth. Bright, passionate red.

"You'll ruin my gown."

"I love your gown. Let's take it off."

Lucy laughed again. "You're bad."

"No. *You're* bad." Seth let her up, and shook his head in dismay. Lucy watched his pale green eyes take in the spaghetti straps and form-fitting bodice of her dress, then followed the movement of his gaze down the tight skirt and along the train that trailed at least eight feet behind her. She could swear she saw his mouth water.

"There's more material in your train than in your actual dress." He shook his head again. "What is your dad going to say when he sees that gown?"

"Oh, he may reprimand me when he sees me, but it will be for show. I'm guessing he's already seen and approved the dress."

Seth laughed. "And I guess I have to get accustomed to the fact that he'll know everything we do."

"Sometimes before we even know we're going to do it. His sources are very good."

Seth suddenly became serious. This time when he put his arm around Lucy's waist and brought her to him, his green eyes were intense with emotion. "As long as he doesn't try to keep us apart."

Lucy smiled and slowly traced the shape of his perfect

mouth with her fingertip. "I don't think we'll have to worry about that. But, even if my father does try something, I won't ever leave you again."

"And I won't ever let you go." They gazed into each other's eyes for a few seconds before Seth kissed her. The meeting of their lips started off slowly but, as always, their chemistry exploded and the kiss seemed to take on a life of its own, deepening before Lucy had a chance to stop it. Tingles of excitement spiraled through her. Her breathing became shallow. Her hands began to lift to Seth's tie. But, luckily, her senses returned.

She pulled away. "Enough!" she scolded, but her voice was filled with laughter. "Mildred's in the living room with Owen! We don't want to scandalize her."

"We're married. We can't create any more scandals. In fact, our only real worry now is to make sure that your father doesn't try to put Owen in purple tights."

"I believe Ty had your lawyers put that stipulation in the agreement he signed with my dad to build his retreat in Little Rock."

Still serious, Seth said, "Who would have ever believed our situation would turn out like this?"

"Mildred. From what I hear from the nanny brigade, she predicted this right from the beginning. She said, Seth Bryant will not let a monarchy take his wife and son. She won fifty bucks from Audrey."

"Audrey never did have enough faith in me."

Lucy laughed again, but she wiggled out of Seth's arms and took her red evening bag from her rose-trimmed vanity. The entire suite was still decorated and furnished the way she had done it as a young, single woman. Now everything would change.

With her back to Seth, she smiled to herself. Everything *had* changed. And so much for the better. She wouldn't live on Xavier Island. She would live in Porter, Arkansas, with her husband who helped run a highly successful business in which he held a one-third ownership. Owen would be raised like an average little boy, except one teacher, one cafeteria worker and two bus drivers in the small-town school would actually be bodyguards employed by Xavier Island. Xavier Island would also pay for two additional policemen to be added to Porter's small force. These policemen were former Secret Service agents. And they would covertly monitor Owen's life. Still, that was much better than Owen being shut up in a castle.

But the best news of all was that King Alfredo had purchased the mortgage on the ranch Cooper Bryant owned and he'd given the mortgage to Seth as a wedding gift. Seth and Ty now had a means to lure Cooper into a discussion. Seth had the opportunity to tell Cooper he was sorry, ask forgiveness and close that chapter of his life.

She turned and smiled at Seth. "Ready to meet your subjects?"

Seth grimaced. "As ready as I'll ever be."

"Good." She kissed his check before tucking her hand beneath his elbow.

Though it was already nearly Thanksgiving, Lucy had a feeling the three Bryant brothers would be back together by Christmas. And be a real family once again. Just like she now had, she thought with a smile.

* * * * *

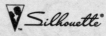

This September,

✓ Silhouette®

SPECIAL EDITION™

brings you the third book in the exciting new continuity

Eleven students.
One reunion.
And a secret that will
change everyone's lives.

THE MEASURE OF A MAN
(SE #1706)
by award-winning author
MARIE FERRARELLA

Jane Johnson had worked at her alma mater for several years before the investigation into her boss, Professor Gilbert Harrison, put her job at risk. Desperate to keep her income, Jane begged her former classmate Smith Parker to help her find secret information that could exonerate the professor. Smith was reluctant—he wanted to stay out of trouble—but he couldn't resist the charms of the beautiful single mom. The hours they spent together soon led to intense sparks…and all-out passion. But when an old secret threatens Smith's job—and his reputation—will the fallout put an end to their happiness forever?

*Don't miss this compelling story—
only from Silhouette Books.*

Available at your favorite retail outlet.